Table of Contents

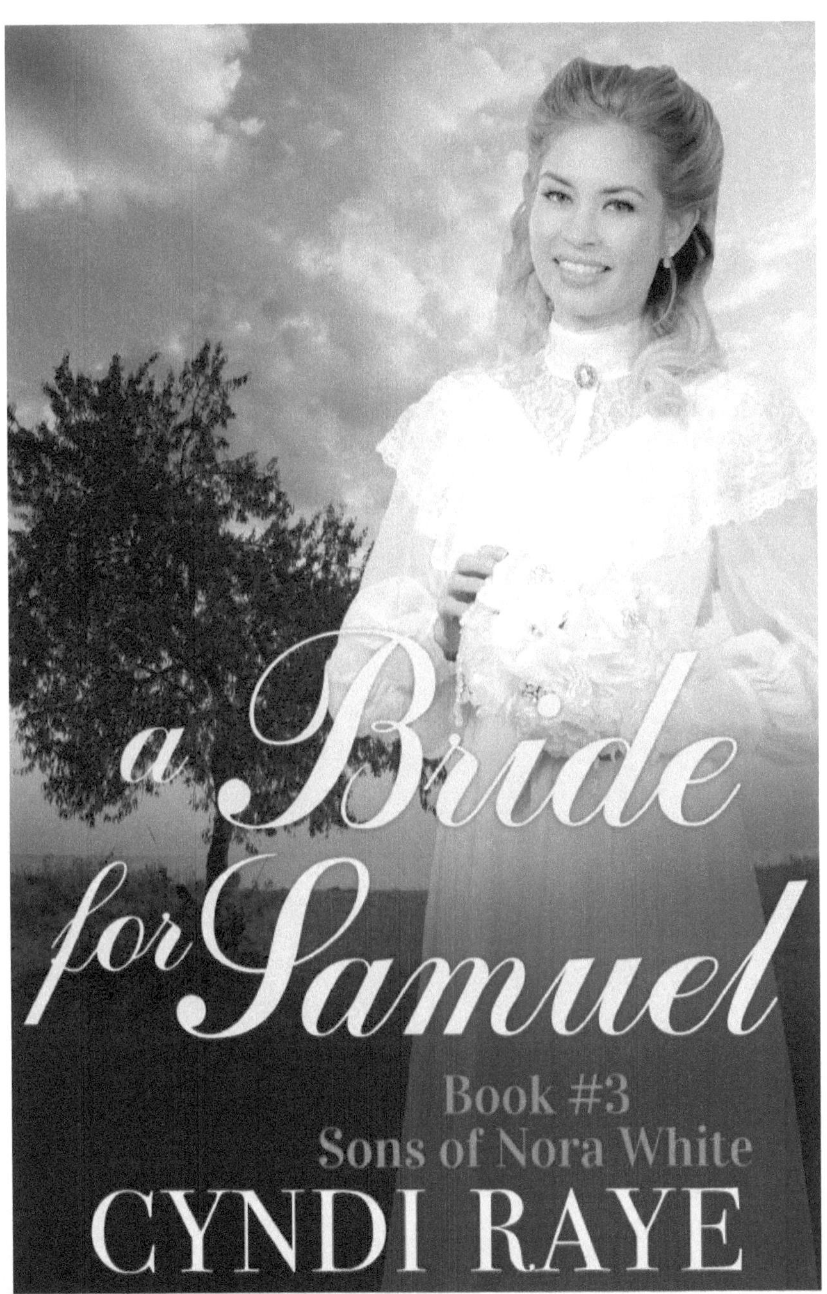

a Bride
for Samuel
Book #3
Sons of Nora White
CYNDI RAYE

A Bride for Samuel

by

Cyndi Raye

Sons Of Nora White

Book #3

---

1. http://www.CyndiRaye.com

Dedication

To CJ, a sweet, happy smiling face that always sweetens the world with her sunshine and laughter. She truly has a rare gift indeed, one that will change the path of each person she meets. Embrace the many adventures in this journey called life.
To our sugar pie honey-bunch, know that we all love you!

***

Author's Note:
I took a little author creative with the history of the North Texas Lunatic Asylum, which was actually built in 1885. Since my stories are in the 1870's, the asylum wasn't built yet in North Texas, only in Austin. This asylum was built North of the Texas and Pacific railway tracks. When the building was opened, only 1/2 of the wings were complete, which would make it easier if Callie had to sneak in and rescue her uncle.

Another thing I learned was about the Poor House or Poor Farms. You may remember your parents or grandparents talking about going to the poorhouse. These were usually farms back in the 1800's and the patients worked for their room and board. There is one story I want to pass on to you. In Texas, if the patient was too lazy to work on the farm, the state gave him a train ticket and cash to get out of Texas to never return! How's that for work ethic?

I hope you enjoy this story of Samuel and Callie!

Chapter 1

Samuel flipped open the pocket watch, then snapped it shut before stuffing it back in his vest. "The train is ten minutes late," he told the pastor's wife, who stood beside him, hands clutched together in annoyance.

Mrs. Conners pursed her lips in an angry fashion. "It's not unusual for the train to run a few minutes late. Perhaps I should go back to the church to prepare for the service."

"It's up to you, but I do appreciate your husband's understanding of our unique situation."

The pastor's wife was always a quiet woman, except for today. She didn't fail to let Samuel know her displeasure. "Sir, you standing in for your brother while he marries someone else is highly unheard of. What if this mail order bride doesn't want you?"

Mrs. Conners sure was blunt. Who knew this little lady had it in her to be so forward speaking? She had always kept to herself, never saying an unkind word during her husband's tenure in Wichita Falls.

He had always thought she was a dignified, shy woman. Now, she was agitated and vocal. Samuel turned to her, tipping his hat. "I'm so sorry, ma'am, but Adam is about to marry his childhood sweetheart. He thought she was out of his reach and agreed to a mail order bride and then, suddenly she was back, and they fell in love all over again. Can you imagine a love so strong to withstand all the years of separation and then suddenly, there they are, face to face?"

Mrs. Conners had a dreamy look on her face, exactly as Samuel had planned. He had gone a bit overboard in theatrics but found it was his duty to make sure nothing stopped Adam and Melody from tying the knot today. It was his brotherly duty.

Just like it was his brotherly duty to marry this mail order bride. Even if he didn't want a bride. Samuel knew it would be his turn next, his Ma had planned for each of her three boys to marry, except he hadn't planned to get married so soon. Actually, if it hadn't been for the circumstances that found Melody and Adam together at last, he had thought about talking his Ma right out of ordering a mail order bride for him.

Samuel didn't want to be tied down to a wife and then have a bunch of little children running around. His oldest brother Luke was waiting for his first child to be born and Samuel figured he'd enjoy having a niece or nephew at the ranch, but for himself, he loved being a free soul. He liked riding the ranch by himself, having a good time with the other ranch hands and living life on the open plains.

Now, he had to marry a complete stranger because he promised his brother's new wife and his Ma he'd do it so Adam and Melody could be together.

He'd do anything for his family. Even marry someone he didn't want to marry. How horrible will his life be now? He flipped open the watch again, getting more agitated. The only reason he agreed was because of the clause in the marriage contract that gave them both a three month trial to change their minds. Samuel was determined in those three months he'd make sure to be the worst husband ever. His bride would be happy to high-tail it far from the White Ranch by the time he was done with her.

No way was he going to stay tied down. His young life was only beginning. Adam and Luke were willing to settle down to a mundane life with a wife and kids. Not Samuel, no sir! He wanted fun, excitement and to sow his wild oats. Even though he wasn't sure what that entailed, he still planned to sow them!

A rumble began under his boots as the train's whistle was heard in the distance. The pastor's wife took his arm, afraid of falling from the constant shaking movement. "It looks like she's here," Samuel announced.

Mrs. Conners nodded, grasping onto his arm with her other hand. She didn't come to the depot often and wasn't prepared for all the racket a train made. When Samuel had explained to Pastor Conner the circumstances of needing a marriage ceremony right away, he had asked his wife to go to the station to make sure the bride-to-be was comfortable with the changes. Hence, the pastor's wife hanging onto his arm like it was a fence post sticking out of the ground.

Passengers scurried off the train, dust covering their faces and clothing, dresses wrinkled and dishevelled. Samuel waited until the very last person got off and then looked around for the bride.

"Wonder where she got to?" he muttered.

"Right here's where I got to. You must be the phenomenal Mr. White. Well, hello, how do you do? I am the future Mrs. White."

A slim hand slaked out from a person in a pair of strange looking trousers and a button down baggy shirt. The trousers were held up by a pair of suspenders while a black sack coat covered a slim body from shoulders to thighs. Samuel never saw blue pants before!

The pastor's wife gasped. She clutched tighter on Samuel's arm, pulling him closer. "What is that?"

Samuel shook his head, a grin spreading over his face. "I have no idea?"

"I am Callie Johnson, the future Mrs. White. Please ignore the lack of dress, I am undercover."

Samuel looked into the bluest pair of eyes he had ever seen. They were filled with humor as if she enjoyed shocking others with her strange clothing. "Undercover?"

She nodded. "Yes, I'll explain after we are married."

Samuel thought the pastor's wife would faint dead away. He moved to the bench and forced her to sit. "Take a breather, I'll find out what is going on?"

After settling Mrs. Conners and prying her hands from his arm, he turned back to the woman wearing men's clothing. "You say you are in disguise? Before we become man and wife, I'm going to need to know why you are undercover?"

She pulled off the black wool hat, it's wide, flat brim hiding the fact there was a beautiful woman underneath with perfect creamy skin. Her blonde wavy locks spilled out and fell across her shoulders. She pushed them back with a slim hand. She gave him the brightest, widest smile he ever saw. It made him want to smile right back but he had to be stern, didn't he? This was not what he had expected in a bride!

"Mr. White, it is imperative I marry immediately, if not sooner. Do you have everything prepared?"

Samuel was dumbfounded. He was asking her questions and she was throwing other ones right back at him. It made no sense. He answered anyway. "We'll be going to the church and getting married right away. It doesn't look as if you are prepared for a wedding ceremony, I'm afraid. Would you care to clean up and change?"

The woman looked appalled. "There's no time for changing. We must be married right away."

Samuel scratched his head, puzzled. "Well, that's fine if you want to wear those things but I ain't never seen blue pants before."

Callie flung her head back, revealing a milky white neck and laughed out loud. She slapped her hand across her thigh. "That's because they are a brand new invention." She slid her hand through Samuel's arm. "Let's get to the church and I'll explain on the way."

Samuel held out his other hand for Mrs. Conner, helping both ladies from the platform. Once they were all on steady ground, he inclined his head towards his new strange bride-to-be. "I'm listening," he told her with a grin.

"A man named Levi Strauss invented these and calls them blue jeans. Why, in San Francisco, the gold miners were flocking to buy these durable copper riveted jeans because they have deep pockets to keep the gold from falling out. I sound like an advertisement for the blue jeans, oh dear!" She giggled to herself at such a thought.

"You come from San Francisco then?" He had no clue where Miss Addie found this woman! She sure was a strange one but she made him smile. Her soft hand lying on his arm felt nice, real nice. When she spoke, she turned and looked right at him as if he were the most important person in her line of vision.

"Mr. White, I have a story to tell you that will shake the very ground you walk on. I am not from San Francisco but my uncle and my father were gold mining a few years back. That's all I can say now because we need to get to the church."

He helped the two ladies in the wagon and they made their way towards the church. After helping them down from the bench, he turned to follow the pastor's wife inside, allowing Miss Johnson to go ahead of him. Samuel wondered if the pastor would even agree to marry the two of them. Why, a woman wearing improper wedding material had to be scandalous, wasn't it?

Samuel wasn't certain himself if he wanted to marry her!

Yet, he had promised his Ma and Melody that he would do so, even if he planned to have the marriage annulled in three months. He remembered how Luke planned to arrange an annulment at first until his oldest brother fell in love with Abigail.

Samuel glanced over at the woman walking down the isle with him. What was he going to do with a woman wearing pants? Why was she wearing such odd clothing? He leaned in, whispering so she was the only person to hear his words. "I must tell you the truth. You came to marry my brother Adam but his childhood sweetheart came back and he is marrying her today at our ranch. I have agreed to step in and honor the agreement. However, I can only give you three months, Miss Johnson. Have you read the clause in the marriage contract?"

She seemed surprised at his words, then she turned and smiled, her little perky nose lifting up in the air as they made their way closer to the front of the church. "I'm sorry to hear this but nothing surprises or shocks me! You should know I read every contract I willingly sign. Now, Mr. White, It doesn't matter which brother I marry and if it's the only way to make you marry me today, right now, I will agree to three months, but as I said in the letter sent earlier this month, I have no intention of retracting the marriage contract if you chose to have me. After we are married today there may be a few teeny, tiny favors I will ask of you. It's why this marriage is so very important for me right now. If you are fine with these tiny issues and details, then I will agree to whatever you want."

He grinned then broke into a wide smile. This was too easy! "Are you saying you will agree to annul the marriage in three months time and give me back my wonderful freedom?"

"Yes, of course."

"Why not then!" He walked her to the front of the church where Pastor Conner and two witnesses stood. The pastor stared at Callie Johnson for a moment or two then opened his tattered bible and lowered his head mumbling something about judging others and Jesus.

"We are gathered here today to witness the marriage of Samuel White and his mail order bride, uh, name please?"

"Miss Callie Johnson."

Samuel tuned the pastor out, instead thinking of the woman who stood beside him, her hand gently resting on his arm. Who was this lady? She was beautiful, even if the clothes she wore spoke of secrets and mystery. Perhaps he should have demanded she reveal her hidden agenda. Except he knew all about secrets, so if she didn't want to discuss them yet, he was obliged to respect her wishes. The good Lord above knew he had his own secrets.

She had taken the stiff, wide-brimmed hat off, making it obvious there was definitely a woman underneath those britches, or, as she called them, blue jeans. Samuel smirked at the thought, causing the pastor to stop in mid-sentence.

"You alright there, Mr. White?"

Samuel cleared his throat. "Uh, yes. Continue, please, my apologies."

Instead of becoming upset at his interruption, Callie Johnson elbowed him in the ribs which make him jump. He turned to see a slight smile on her profile. He grinned and turned away before the preacher took notice.

"I now pronounce you husband and wife, you may kiss the bride."

Samuel had no problem with this part of the ceremony. He placed his arms around her and pulled her slim figure towards him. She rested against his chest, her hands lying flat against his shirt. Samuel leaned down, watching her reaction.

Her head was tilted back, her eyes half closed, her hair falling in waves down her back over his arms. Samuel leaned in and gave her a kiss right on her plush mouth. As soon as their lips touched he pressed her closer, kissing her more fiercely as if he wasn't able to get enough of her sweetness.

Someone called out. "Dear God in heaven!"

Another witness protested.

"Oh, my! Please, stop!"

Callie pushed away from him, a surprised look on her face. "Why, Mr. White, you sure are a fine kisser!" Her voice shot out across the church, causing the pastor's wife to gasp again before lifting the bunch of flowers in her hand over the bottom part of her face. It almost looked as if Mrs. Conner was smiling.

Samuel felt about ten feet tall. He liked how she complimented him on their first kiss. He brushed a hand across his brow, not quite sure what to do next. So he told her what was on his mind. "Well, Mrs. White, I'd say you are quite the fine kisser yourself!"

She blushed before turning to the pastor. "Pastor Conner, thank you for marrying us on such short notice. Now, we have to get going."

There was no hurry to get back to the ranch except for the wedding of his brother and Melody. Since the train was late to begin with, his brother was probably already married by now. He figured they'd miss the wedding but he was doing his brother a favor by marrying the mail order bride. They would take their time and enjoy the day.

Boy, and what a day it was turning out to be! What a fine wife she would be. As they left the church she asked him, "Can we get a bite to eat before we start our journey to your ranch and then I'll explain those teeny, tiny favors to you."

Samuel was anxious to hear what she had to say. Jenna's café was right down the street, so they slipped inside and got a table near the back. Most of the diners were sitting far enough away they could speak without interruption.

"Well, well, well, I hear we have a new bride and groom. Congratulations are in order. The meal is on me."

Samuel turned to see Miss Jenna striding towards them. If anyone knew what was happening in this town, it was her. She seemed to know everybody's business even before it happened. How she stayed single so long was beyond him. He had tried flirting with her several times but she always shot him down and put him in his place. She was from the big city before opening her eating establishment in Wichita Falls.

Jenna didn't take any sass in her cafe. Everyone in town and who came to town learned that about her. He smiled when he saw her. "Morning, Miss Jenna. We'll have a hearty breakfast and some coffee to boot."

Jenna nodded his way before turning to his new wife. "Welcome to Wichita Falls, Mrs. White."

"Why, thank you. It's a pleasure to be here."

Jenna grinned. "That wedding outfit is sure to be the town gossip today."

Callie lifted her chin and smiled away, showing bright, even teeth. Her smile was infectious. "I'm sure it will and that's what I do best, leave a trail of gossip in my wake." She shrugged as if it didn't make no difference who spoke ill of her.

"I'm pleased to meet someone who doesn't give a fig about gossip. I'll be right back with your order."

While they waited on breakfast, Samuel noticed how his new wife watched the small Chinese family through the big picture window. They were staring at the patrons inside and looked hungry. After a few minutes, the head of the family came inside, holding a small bottle, using hand signals to try to speak to the waitress.

"Will you excuse me, please?" Callie stood and walked over to the little Chinese man and began to speak in his native language. Samuel was dumbstruck as she held a very meaningful conversation with the stranger. His wife knew Chinese? What else did she know?

Within minutes, she explained to the waitress what he wanted to order and stood with him while they packed it up so he was able to take it along. She motioned and pointed towards the outside while they spoke for some time. Then the Chinese man bowed to Callie and then handed her the strange bottle before he left the café.

She sat back down, placing the bottle on the table. "I'm sorry, I didn't meant to take so long," she told him, smiling away as if she didn't just speak a foreign language to a little man.

"You speak Chinese?"

"Why, yes, I do. I learned the language when my father and uncle were in California. I was a child then but we were surrounded by so many Chinese at the mines, I was fortunate to befriend a family who spoke broken English and were willing to teach me a thing or two."

"So, you are a miner's daughter?"

"Was. Those days are long gone. My father and uncle bought a ranch a few hours from here. Well, there's the story I'm about to enlighten you with. But first, as a thank-you, we must try Mr. Wong's Medicinal Wine."

"It's a bit early don't you think?" Samuel was all for a sip of wine now and again but mostly he took a slug from the whiskey bottle when they were playing cards in the barn. He never drank first thing in the morning.

"If you take a look out the window you will see Mister and Misses Wong watching to make sure we accept their gift. They are thanking me for what I did for them. It would be rude of us not to taste their wine."

"Well, sure, if you say so." Samuel reached across the table and pulled the cap from the strange bottle. He took a sniff. "It doesn't smell too bad."

"It's yellow rice wine. They soak herbs and other things to get that flavor. Try a sip."

"Right from the bottle?"

"Yes."

Samuel lifted the bottle to his mouth, taking a small sip. He was surprised it tasted so good. "Not bad," he mentioned, handing the bottle to Callie.

She accepted the bottle, raising it to the window and nodding to the Chinese family standing outside. She also drank straight from the bottle like he had. "Your quite the lady," Samuel told her.

He almost laughed out loud when her face puckered up but he could tell she was trying to force it down without insulting Mister Wong. Samuel took the bottle and drank more so she didn't have to. "It is an acquired taste," he told her. With just two small sips a warmth spread through his whole body from the top of his head to the tips of his boots.

A moment later their breakfast was set on the table. Samuel was enjoying the Chinese medicinal wine so he didn't eat too much while Callie cleaned her plate.

She wiped at her mouth with a cloth napkin and grinned. "You may want to slow down a little, else it will hit you all at once. I've seen it before with the toughest of men."

Maybe she was right but he wasn't about to give up a good thing. "I'm fine," he told her. "It's not like I never drank before."

Callie stared at him. "I hope it's okay to call you Samuel since we are married now."

"Sure, and I'll call you Callie. Now, we best be on our way to the ranch so we can at least catch the last of the celebration of my brother's wedding."

Samuel paid the bill, guiding Callie outside. He blinked several times but the whole street seemed fuzzy. She slid her arm through his. "Don't try to fight it, Samuel. You've had a bit too much to drink. May I have that bottle please?"

Samuel didn't realize he had been holding onto the small bottle as if it were a gold nugget. "Sure," he said but held onto it. His mouth was numb, more so than after a few sips of whiskey while playing cards.

Callie led them to a horse tied at the post in front of the Café. "Here we are."

"Wait, where is the wagon?" Samuel squinted his eyes, looking around for the wagon. "I know I brought it this morning before picking you up? Where did I place that darn thing?" His mouth didn't want to cooperate as he leaned into Callie.

"Don't you worry none. I traded with the Chinese family. All they had was this one horse to travel to the next town and those children, poor things, had to walk. You saw them."

Samuel was no longer steady on his feet. "You traded our wagon and horse for a single horse? We'll honey, you sure are being kind with my belongings!"

Callie leaned in to whisper in his ear. "I am sorry, truly, but I promise to pay you back tenfold. Now, we better get to your ranch."

It took Samuel awhile longer than necessary to get on the saddle but he did so and held out his arm to lift Callie up. Instead of swinging herself in front of him, she whipped her leg across the back, then wrapped her arms around his waist, her whole body tight up against him. How in the world was he going to concentrate with her so darn close?

As they rode out of town, several onlookers stared at the two. "I believe we'll be the talk of the town," Samuel slurred. He lifted the bottle to his mouth again, taking a much needed sip.

Callie laughed out loud. "Mr. White, I don't much care what anyone thinks. Do you? Besides, there is one thing on my mind right now and it isn't what this town thinks."

"You sure are a sweet thing, honey. What is that one thing you have on your mind?" He was hoping it was letting him take her in his arms and kissing her sweet lips again.

She placed her mouth near his left ear, her warm breath dancing across his skin. "Remember the teeny, tiny favor I need help with?"

"You never did say what it was."

"That's because it is so important to me that I'd do anything, including marry a man I didn't know to accomplish what I need done."

Samuel reached back and patted her arm. "Aww, honey, you just ask and it's yours." He wished the darn horse would go faster, he was anxious to get back to the ranch. The spots in front of his eyes weren't helping any. Good thing it wasn't too difficult to guide a horse.

"I'm so happy to hear you say those words. Well, then, after we get back to your ranch we need to devise a strategy, a plan of action of sorts for our adventure."

"An adventure? I love the ranch and everything it stands for but living a mundane life on the ranch with a woman who harps at me isn't what I relish, so tell me about this adventure."

Callie laughed out loud. "Well, sir, we are about to break my Uncle Jessie out of the North Texas Lunatic Asylum!"

Chapter 2

Callie wasn't expecting such a handsome man for a husband. Even if he was a bit tipsy from the Chinaman's Medicinal Wine, his smile was genuine and his demeanor attractive. She probably could've stopped him after a few sips but the thought of explaining her mission to a total stranger was uttermost on her mind. She hadn't paid attention before it was too late and he had drank more than half the bottle.

Her arms were wrapped around his waist. He was so muscular. Strong, handsome and adventurous was exactly what she needed in a partner to help break out her uncle from that awful place. Once Uncle Jessie was out of danger, she would be able to reveal herself and claim back their land.

"Did you just say what I thought you said?"

She nodded even though he wasn't able to see. "I did, and I have an idea of how to go about arranging the escape."

"Are you for real?" he asked her, his head loping from one side to the other. She was afraid Samuel would have a headache after the rice wine wore off. She had seen it many times growing up. It was why she forced herself to take only one sip and that almost made her gag but she didn't want to offend Mister Wong and his wife.

"I am real and your wife of exactly one hour and fifty minutes."

"How do you know how long we've been married?"

She snapped the pocket watch closed and stuffed it back in the pocket of his vest before smiling. He never even noticed she had pulled it out. He was more intoxicated than she originally thought. "I just checked your pocket watch," she told him. It was time to be honest with him but he needed to get home and sleep off the wine first. The stuff was potent and she wished now she'd paid more attention to how much he drank.

Meanwhile, there was no point in letting the awful things that had happened interfere with her wedding day. A day she never should've had to be forced to do but if it freed her uncle then that's all that mattered.

"Another twenty minutes or so and we'll be at the White Ranch. You'll love my brothers and their wives. Oh, and my Ma, Nora. She's the one who concocted this whole mail-order bride stuff."

"I'm anxious to meet them all," she told him, shouting a little louder as the horse clip-clopped down the road, his hooves making noise over the stones. A small Texas breeze whipped through the air. "Tell me about your family," she urged. Maybe getting him to talk more would sober him up. It was a long shot but she was desperate to explain what she needed from him and wanted his full attention when she did so.

"Well, there is the three of us. Luke, he's the oldest. He married the first mail-order bride, Abigail. My brother wasn't planning to stay married because of the secret. As you know the contract says we can get an annul, uh, a, annulling, oh, jeez, annul the marriage in three months if the bride is not to our satisfaction. The problem with that is we have to keep our hands to ourselves. No marriage bed stuff if you know what I mean."

Callie shook her head, not taking offence at his words since she was the cause of his drunkenness. His words were becoming more slurred by the minute. There was no sobering him up at this rate. She took the bottle from his hand, not realizing he was still sipping on it. She had to focus and pay attention!

"That's enough of the Chinese Medicinal Wine, Samuel."

Samuel laughed at everything she said from there on in. He stumbled over his words about his middle brother Adam and the best friend who was becoming his wife today. He'd never be able to help her plan out her uncle's escape in this condition. There was no sense in even trying to get his help today. It would have to wait until morning.

She may as well enjoy the merriment at the reception when they got to the ranch. With all the worrying she had done in the last few months, it wouldn't hurt to be able to relax among people who weren't trying to cause her harm. Since they would be at a wedding reception, perhaps no one would notice her husband was extremely drunk.

<><>

A sign hung from the large open gate, swinging gently back and forth. It read White Ranch in big, bold letters, some beginning to fade from the elements. By now, Samuel was slumped back against Callie as she had took over the reins. The horse seemed as wobbly as Samuel as they went down the single lane leading to the ranch. It was a wonder Samuel remembered the way home.

In the yard a celebration was going on as people mingled about. She was nervous meeting the rest of the family but made up her mind to focus on the reason she was here.

"We're home, darling." Samuel hiccuped several times.

"Samuel, perhaps you don't want to say much right now. Your family will notice you had too much to drink."

He shrugged, taking the reins from her hands. "Let's ride in like we are saving the day, you know how the cowboy saves the lady."

Before Callie was able to respond, Samuel nudged the horse as he gave a holler. The horse took off as she tightened her hold on his waist as they flew down the road. She had to admit, he was a fascinating man. He rode a horse like it was naturally a part of him, even if he was a bit tipsy. Well, a lot tipsy.

The ride was exhilarating, just what she needed. Callie flung her head back, holding onto his waist with one hand while clutching the top of her hat with the other. "Yes! This is so much fun!"

Samuel laughed out loud.

Callie hung on for dear life, her smile widening as he raced towards the yard.

A crowd began to gather, looks of surprise on their faces. Callie knew her blue jeans would be the first shocking thing they noticed but she didn't care. Being with Samuel and knowing he was her husband was all she needed. She just hoped the rest of his family would understand.

An older man with bright red hair stood on one end of the crowd, his hat in one hand. A tall woman with dark brown hair neatly coiled on her head stood beside him. She wore a neat blue dress and a serious look on her face. Callie had a feeling she was the notorious Nora White, matron of the family.

Samuel started to laugh again, causing a rippling effect as Callie joined in. The horse was slowing down but with all the Hollerith Samuel was doing it was a wonder he hadn't scared the poor horse.

Before Callie realized, they had come to a complete stop in front of a group of people who were staring with both shocked and amused looks on their faces.

So she gave them the biggest smile ever!

"Samuel! What is the meaning of this?"

Samuel lifted a hand and waved to the woman in the blue dress. "Ma! I'm back with my wife, C, Call, Calliope, uh, Callie! Yes, her name is Callie and I've just had the best darn Chinese wine ever!"

One of the men stood with his hands on his hips, a beautiful woman at his side. "Samuel, you're drunk!"

Samuel nodded and then let out the biggest guffaw the others ever heard coming from the youngest White son. The crowd chuckled, some outright laughing along with him, not knowing why they did. One couple slipped away, most likely the groom Callie was set to marry before Samuel came along and interrupted.

The two looked perfect for each other. She was a beautiful bride with long wavy hair flowing down her back. She placed a hand on her husband's chest as if they belonged together. Although the groom seemed more serious than she'd ever think possible, Callie turned her head away, knowing it was a private moment, one she didn't need to watch.

There were more urgent things at hand, like getting Samuel off this horse.

Everyone continued to stare at Callie as if they were trying to figure out who or what she was. It occurred to her just then she probably looked like a boy with her pants on and her legs dangling on either side of this horse.

So she picked up the rim of her hat and lifted it in the air as her golden locks escaped from the wool hat. They fell around her shoulders as some of the ladies in the crowd gasped. "Hello everyone. It's a pleasure to meet you. I'm the new Mrs. White!"

"Yeehaw!" Samuel yelled, even louder than he had been on their way here. He took his hat off and threw it in the air. "Guess what. We are going on an adventure!"

Nora White crossed her arms over her chest. "And, pray tell, what exactly do you mean by an adventure, son?"

He guffawed again. "Well, Ma, I'm going to help Mrs. White here break out her uncle from the North Texas Lunatic Asylum!"

The crowd went silent at his announcement.

He slid from the horse and almost lost his balance. Callie watched as his brother moved forward to steady Samuel. "I believe it's time for a nap."

Callie immediately slid down, went to her new husband and wrapped an arm around the other side of him. They each held onto him as he stumbled towards the main house. Nora White followed along, not saying a word.

Callie felt eyes on her from behind. She wasn't sure if they were friendly or angry but she wasn't about to turn around to find out. She'd have to explain everything soon but her most important job was to make sure Samuel was taken care of. She was his wife after all and wasn't going to ignore that fact even if all she wanted was to free her uncle from that horrible place.

Luke settled his little brother in one of the rooms upstairs, while Callie stood in the kitchen, hat in hand. What now, she thought to herself. Would Nora White throw her out?

"Callie? Will you have some tea with me?" Nora began to place two cups on the kitchen table, as if it hadn't been a question but an order.

"Thank you, Mrs. White." Callie sat down, ready to hear a lecture or whatever the mother of a mail order bride's husband did in a situation like this.

The gaiety of the evening drifted through the open door. Nora noticed, closed the door and sat down, muffling some of the noise. After taking a sip of tea, she looked at Callie over the brim of her teacup. "I'm sure there is a story behind what I just witnessed and I've plenty of time to listen."

Nora didn't make her feel as if she were a horrible person, at least that was a relief. Callie sighed. "I apologize for Samuel's behavior. It is my fault."

"Oh? How so?"

"I was so busy thinking of other things I forgot to make sure he only took a few sips of the Medicinal Wine. It was given to us as a thank you from a Chinese family."

"I see. How nice to receive a gift." Nora placed her cup on the table.

"Well, it was for the wagon. I suppose I am sorry about giving away a wagon, also."

Nora snorted. "You gave away our horse and wagon? Is this the reason the two of you came here on one lonely horse?"

Callie nodded. "I'm afraid so."

Nora picked up her tea cup again even if she didn't drink from it. Looking over the brim, Callie noticed a small smile spreading across her face.

"Looking back I guess I am sorry about that, too. The Chinese family only had one poor horse to get to their cousin's house in Dallas.

Those poor children had to walk. I was so disturbed by this I offered our wagon in exchange for their horse and they returned the favor with a bottle of their best medicinal wine. I probably didn't have the right to do so. I jumped in and tried to help but obviously, I've overstepped my boundaries."

Nora smiled. "So, it seems you are used to helping others?"

"Yes, on our ranch there was always some type of charity work to do. Oh, I've said too much!"

Nora patted Callie's hand. "I think we will get along fine. I'm not sure why you want to break your uncle out of the lunatic asylum or why he is even there, but I'm sure there is good reason to do so and we'll worry about that tomorrow. You said *your* ranch. Tell me about it."

"Yes, let's hear all about it," Luke chimed in, taking a chair at the table.

The front door pushed open as the red-haired older man shuffled through to the table. "May as well tell us all about it," he told her, taking a seat.

Callie looked around. This family was tight-knit. She hoped they would understand her wish to set her uncle free.

"Wait! I'm coming back down!" Samuel stood at the top of the stairs, teetering back and forth. Two chairs slid back as the men stood, ready to help him. He waved them away. "I'm sobering up, no worry at all."

It took Samuel five minutes to get to the table while everyone watched. Finally, Luke went over and grabbed his arm. "If you are so determined to be here, then sit down. He pulled out a chair, making sure Samuel was seated.

Callie was aware of every cyngle pair of eyes on her, even Samuels. His were filled with merriment even if he was drunker than a skunk.

She pulled her shoulders up and took a deep breath. "I'm sorry to intrude on your kindness but I was invited here by way of becoming a mail order bride. So, saying that, I hope you understand that I accepted the position for a specific reason."

"We understand, now let's get to the meat of the problem," Nora told her. She obviously didn't like to dally.

Callie hid her hands on her lap underneath the table. They shook slightly as she tried to explain the last six months of her life. "My father, Jeremiah Johnson, and Uncle Jess worked the mines in California, making them wealthy men. There was a third brother who didn't go along. He wasn't left out, he was lazy. When my father and uncle came back to Texas they bought some land and started a ranch."

Samuel's eyes were on her and she looked into them. Intoxicated or not, it seemed as if he encouraged her with his intent gaze. "My mother died in childbirth having me and last year my father passed away."

"I'm so sorry, dear," Nora told her.

"We are sorry," Luke added. His wife, Abigail, had come in and taken a seat next to her husband. She reached out to pat Callie's hand as well.

"Thank you. My uncle and I were perfectly fine working the ranch but the third brother, the lazy one, demanded to be a partner without doing any of the work. He had stayed away all those years and then suddenly wanted in. When Uncle Jessie refused to make him a partner, Uncle Jacob tried to kidnap me to force a ransom. All he cared about was the money, not the ranch."

"Kidnap his own niece! What kind of man is he?" Luke growled.

Nora gasped.

Samuel watched her closely. "How did he kidnap you?"

"I'm afraid he didn't. He never knew who I was so I hid whenever he came to the Double J. One time he came asking the ranch hands where to find me. It goes to show he didn't even know what I looked like because that time I stood almost in front of him and he never recognized I was his niece. Then he tried to bribe a few of our men, offering to pay cash to kidnap me. They were loyal and sent him on his way."

"Oh, dear! I'm glad you weren't kidnapped," Nora told her.

Luke and Rusty nodded while Samuel, his elbows on the table while he cupped his face in his hands, smiled. "I doubt anyone could capture you." His eyes stared into hers. Callie swallowed. This side of Samuel was quite different. His fun-loving style was replaced by a man who stared at her so intently she wasn't quite sure what to make of things.

Nora coughed softly. "Go on, dear, tell us the rest."

Callie nodded. "Hence the blue jeans."

Rusty scratched his head. "The what?"

"My apparel. I am wearing a pair of what Californians call blue jeans. These are men's britches and are made for the coal mines because they are so durable. My uncle sent away for some to fit me and I worked the ranch in disguise as a boy in case my bad uncle tried to kidnap me again. It was the best secret ever until things got more serious."

"It doesn't look like he succeeded."

"No, but he kept coming around. So, Uncle Jessie was afraid I'd be found out, so he faked my death, put up a gravestone on the family cemetery. My uncle feared for my safety even if I was dressed like a boy. So he sent me to a friend of his in Dallas for awhile."

"I'm so sorry, Callie. I may call you Callie now that you are my newest daughter-in-law?"

Callie smiled at Nora. "Of course. I was only there about three weeks when one of the ranch hands came with bad news. Uncle Jacob had somehow forced his way onto the ranch, took Uncle Jessie to the North Texas Lunatic Asylum and had him committed. I'm sure he gave him something to make him go along willingly because there is no way Uncle Jessie would go without a fight."

Callie was almost in tears thinking about her uncle in that horrible place.

"Is this why you want to break him out?"

"I know that sounds awful but the moment I heard, I travelled to the asylum and demanded to speak to the doctors there. They listened to my story and allowed me to visit with my uncle but because I was not a married woman they would not let me take him out."

Samuel was listening intently. "What does your uncle have to say about the whole thing?"

Callie shook her head. "I'll have you know my uncle can be quite a pistol and he wasn't going to be polite to anyone. He screamed obscenities the whole time I was there. As of right now, they have him in one of those awful rooms where he doesn't see the light of day. He can't come out unless he is wearing what they call a straight jacket, where they bind his hands inside of this awful contraption. It's terrible."

"Is there a reason he is in a lunatic asylum, Callie?" Nora's words were gentle but Callie knew what she meant.

Callie let the tears run down her face. "Uncle Jessie is somewhat crazier than a hog running wild. He is quite eccentric and does what he wants when he wants and doesn't take any sass from no one, so I'm not sure if you want to call that crazy but I love him to pieces. He is bold and wild and says what is on his mind. The doctors at the asylum say he's out of hand. They insist he has a mental disorder and needs restrained. I say it is nonsense."

"Kind of like you? Bold and wild and say what's on your mind? I don't call that crazy, I call it appealing." She knew Samuel was teasing but thinking of her uncle had the tears flowing.

"I guess if the apple doesn't fall far from the tree then I'm crazy as well."

Nora stood. "I have my doubts about anyone here being crazy. I think we need to devise a plan to have your uncle removed from the asylum. Everyone is tired, now let's go out and enjoy the rest of the evening with our guests. Tomorrow we'll be fresh and can discuss this in its entirety. Agreed?"

Heads nodded up and down. "I'll fill in Adam and Melody in the morning, that's if we see them at all tomorrow." Luke pushed his chair back, taking Abigail's hand as they left the kitchen.

Nora walked outside with Rusty at her elbow. Callie sat there, Samuel across from her, his intense gaze starting to wear her down. "Samuel, will you please stop looking at me like that!"

He smiled, lifting a brow. "Like this?" He did it again.

Callie stood, stretching her legs. "Yes, like that. It's been such a long day."

"I agree. Let's go have some of the delicious food outside and I'll introduce you to the others."

Callie was concerned he was still drunk. "Are you okay to move around? You were quite wobbly before."

"It's starting to wear off but I'm afraid I'll need to lean on you just a bit." Samuel stood up, pretending to wobble when he reached out to Callie. She giggled and took his arm, helping to steer him out of the house.

After they mingled with some of the visitors, Samuel filled two plates and they sat down on a bench to eat.

"This is nice, it makes me miss the Double J even more."

"Double J, is the name of your ranch?"

"Yes, named for my father and uncle, Jeremiah and Jessie, respectively."

"Then you will like it here, Callie. I'm glad we met and you're here."

Samuel's words meant the world to her. Here she was with complete strangers trying to convince her new husband to help her break someone out of a horrible place. "I'm sorry to be asking you or your family to help commit a crime. The doctor there won't listen to me, I tried to get him out of my own accord but was helpless. A single lady has limitations they said."

"You are still a relative?"

"If I am a married woman, he would be under the care of my husband, so that's why I decided to go ahead and do the mail order bride agreement. I'm sorry to have deceived you and yet I'm not. I'm desperate for help. My uncle means the world to me and doesn't belong in a lunatic asylum. I was hoping to go explain to them one more time with a husband in tow. If that doesn't work, well, then, we have to break him out."

Samuel placed his arm around her shoulder. "I would do the same thing if it were my family. Since he is now my family, then yes, I'll consider helping your uncle get released from the North Texas Lunatic Asylum!"

Callie rested her head on his shoulder. It felt nice not to be alone. Even if it were a fake marriage with a different agenda. He didn't want to stay married and she needed this marriage to hopefully get her uncle out.

Besides, there was the bit she didn't mention about the buried gold.

Chapter 3

Samuel arrived downstairs later than usual. His head pounded so bad, he was sure it would split in half. Then he remembered how he had drank all the wine given to them from the Chinaman. Everything else last evening was a bit fuzzy, although he did remember speaking with Callie right before he went to bed.

"Little brother looks a bit under the weather this morning," Luke announced in a louder than usual tone. Samuel slapped both hands over his ears.

"Stop talking!"

Luke laughed again, even louder.

Samuel made his way to stand behind his chair, bowing his head to say a last minute prayer before sitting at his place at the table. The others had already started, ignoring his presence except for a nod here and there. As soon as the ranch hands finished up, they excused themselves, wanting to get the day started. Breakfast was a fast meal and these men worked hard at their jobs. Rusty burped, excused himself and followed the others outside a bit slower but determined to start the day early.

That left Nora, Luke, Abigail and his new wife, Callie at the table. Ma must've placed her in one of his brothers old rooms. "Callie, good morning," he addressed her.

She seemed quiet this morning, perhaps a bit tired. Until she smiled, then it lit up her whole face as she gave him one of the brightest smiles he'd ever seen. He returned the greeting.

Nora watched the exchange before finishing her breakfast. "I see you are not spry this morning, Samuel. We need you awake to discuss the plans for the retrieval of Mr. Johnson." She placed a hot, steaming cup of coffee at his place setting. "Drink up."

"Thanks, Ma. I'd like to apologize for coming home the way I did."

Nora patted his shoulder, taking her place at the head of the table.

"It's water under the bridge. Let's hear from your bride." Nora turned to his wife. "Callie, I'd like to officially welcome you to the White Ranch. I placed you in a separate room from your husband, under the circumstances of last night, I felt separate would be better in his condition."

Callie nodded. "Thank you, ma'am."

Samuel watched her speak to his Ma. His bride sure was pretty first thing in the morning. He wished his head didn't ache so bad. It was hard to have a conversation with this banging going on inside his skull.

Nora turned to him. "Samuel, as you know, there is an issue with your wife's family. We are going to devise a plan to have Mr. Johnson placed in the Samuel White family's protection, which will then become your responsibility since you are the husband."

"Thanks, Ma."

Ma turned to Callie. "I've sent one of our ranch hands with a note to fetch the Sheriff of Mill's Ridge."

Samuel noticed how Callie's whole demeanor changed at the mention of a sheriff. "Why?" Her voice was weak and sounded fearful.

"It sounds like your uncle, the lazy one who took over the Double J is breaking the law. Since there is no real jurisdiction out here, most towns make their own laws. The Sheriff of Mill Ridge knows some Texas Rangers who may be able to help your circumstances."

Samuel had to agree. When Mill Ridge was an outlaw town awhile back, the sheriff rode in and wiped out all the bad men. Now the town was thriving with families and ranches in the surrounding areas. Word had it there was an ex-ranger or two living in those parts. "It won't hurt to have a lawman's opinion," Samuel told Callie. He reached out and placed his hand over hers. "Don't worry, Ma knows what she is doing."

Callie smiled, except it didn't reach her eyes. "I figured if our marriage ruse didn't work, I'd break him out and when we got back to our ranch, Jacob would have no choice but to leave. The ranch hands will help, I'm certain. I'm not sure a Texas Ranger will go along with a break-out."

Samuel shook his head. "Let's see what the law has to say first. We'll keep the breaking him out part out of the conversation."

Nora smiled, changing the subject as if they hadn't been speaking about anything except the weather. Samuel noticed the worry lines crossing his wife's brow. He wanted to help her but his Ma was right. First, they had to speak with experts to see what could be done.

As they were finishing up, Samuel heard his newly married brother Adam speaking to someone outside. He grinned at Luke, who slid his chair back faster than a lightening strike.

Samuel raced out the door, diving from the porch to tackle his newly married brother. Luke slammed into them both, causing the three to be knocked to the ground where they began to roll across the yard like a bunch of unsettled school boys.

"Come inside, Melody! Those three will be out there rolling around for some time."

Samuel heard his Ma calling for Adam's wife. He peeked out from the ground to see Callie with one hand on her hip watching them with a surprised look on her face. Nora leaned over to speak to her and she lifted her face up in the air and laughed out loud. The melody of her sweet laughter rang in his ears. He was so busy looking at her, his brother swooped in and flipped him on his back with a thud.

"Looks like Sammy boy is moonstruck too!"

The three sat in a circle on the ground. With chest's heaving, the men grinned at each other.

Samuel turned to see the ladies make their way back inside.

"See what I mean," Luke pointed out.

Adam agreed. "I do see that now. Interesting. Samuel, I thought you wanted to be a free man, no strings attached?"

Samuel thought so, too. But there was something special about Callie. He shrugged. "I still do."

Luke slapped his leg. "I'll bet within two weeks you'll be smitten with her, if you ain't already."

Adam held out his hand. "Let's bet on that, brother. I'll give it a week."

Adam and Luke stood, shaking hands once they were off the ground. "Let's bet our chores for one day again, like we always do."

"Agreed."

"Samuel, you owe me, make sure I win," Luke told him, pointing to the pistol with a white pearl handle Samuel wore. Luke had given it to him a long time ago. It had been their fathers. Luke had known Samuel wanted it and when he gave it to Samuel, Luke mentioned there was a favor attached.

Adam made his demands. "That's not fair. Samuel, you make sure I win, else, I'll tell Ma how you switch jobs with Roger to get out of Sunday church services."

"Great! Just great!" He loved his brothers but at times they were a pain in his head. Like now, the top of his head pounded. At least the three of them would never reveal the secret that kept them so close all these years. There was only one other person that knew about it. Adam's wife, Melody. She had overheard them and promised to keep it quiet. Since she had been Adam's best friend since they were little, Samuel was pretty sure the secret was safe. If she hadn't said anything after all these years, they would be able to trust her.

That was one of the reasons all three brothers had vowed never to marry, because they were afraid the more people that came into their lives, the secret they had kept hidden all these years would come out. It would devastate Nora if she found out. Now, here they are, all three married.

How did this happen? Would the secret continue to stay safe? It had to. For Nora's sake.

The two brothers left Samuel sitting on the ground holding his head in his hands.

<> <>

The room was filled to capacity. Luke and Abigail, Adam and Melody, Nora, Rusty, Samuel and Callie sat at the kitchen table with their guests. Sheriff Jackson Montana from as far as Wichita Falls had been called in, along with Salem Nightingale, the sheriff of Mill Ridge. They brought two men along that Samuel suspected were Texas Rangers.

He was right. Their large presence took up most of the room. Nora had offered them a seat along the wall. Both sheriffs sat while the two rangers refused. "Thank you, Ma'am. My name is Noah Holloway. I'd rather stand as I can think clearer if I pace, I'm sorry to say."

Nora smiled and nodded.

"Same here. Name's Grant Jennings." Samuel noticed he had a slight limp when he came inside and still refused to take the weight off. The rangers were some tough men.

Salem Nightingale began. "When I got your message, Mrs. White, I knew this was serious business at hand. It's why I contacted Sheriff Montana and these two gentleman, who have worked with the Texas Rangers and continue to do so in certain circumstances."

Samuel kept his eye on Callie. Her face was pale and she was blinking way too much. He gave her hand a squeeze. She turned to him for a moment before the one ranger began to speak.

"Sheriff Montana has hard evidence from some of the ranch hands of the Double J who have complained about their boss. Seems the owner, or the man who claims to be the owner, Jacob Johnson, has been using the Double J as a place to hide other rancher's cattle until he sends them to auction in Kansas."

"A cattle thief?" Callie's eyes widened. "How dare he?"

Montana put up his hand. "He must be in cohorts with other men. Beef is becoming increasingly popular on the east coast and there's a tidy profit to be made. How he is accomplishing this task is what we aim to find out."

"I hope you do. Jacob has destroyed my poor uncle, placing him in a lunatic asylum. If he knew what was going on at his ranch, he'd be horrified."

Grant Jennings, the other ranger, spoke up. "I've seen these kind of antics before. It's hard to get someone out of an asylum once they are placed in by family."

Callie stood. "I am family. He is my uncle."

Grant shook his head. "I'm afraid the chance of getting him out are slim but it won't hurt to try."

Callie nodded. "I'm married now, so he can be placed in my husband's care."

Samuel stood, placing an arm around her shoulders. "I'll do whatever I can to help."

"We all will," Nora told the crowd. "However, this is a serious crime and we have to be careful. We don't know how many people Jacob Johnson has in his pocket. If anyone gets wind we are involved with bringing him down, we all may be in danger."

Sheriff Montgomery nodded. "She's right. It's best if everyone works in pairs. Be alert and careful. If you see someone strange in the area, notify us immediately."

"Aren't we quite far enough away from the Double J Ranch? I mean, they wouldn't send someone all the way down here to retaliate, would they?"

"You don't know my Uncle! Look what he did to Jessie!"

Noah Holloway nodded. "This whole area is on alert as far as the rangers are concerned. This man and his outfit are stealing cattle from ranches hundreds of miles away, so who knows who is involved. It's quite the operation and will take some time to catch everyone. Have you noticed any missing from your ranch?"

Nora shook her head. "No, but we are going to do a head count today just to be sure."

Callie twisted her hands together. Samuel tried to reassure her by pulling her in closer. "We'll get your uncle out, no matter what," he told her.

"I appreciate your kind words. In the meantime, there is no reason not to try to have him placed with us. Maybe he can come here until this whole mess with the cattle rustling blows over."

Nora gave Callie a hug. "Of course he can come here."

Ranger Holloway insisted the visit to the North Texas Lunatic Asylum be done in secret. "We don't want to give the Double J any reason whatsoever to believe Mr. Johnson has been let out to come back to claim his land. Is there any proof he signed over the ranch to his brother, Miss White?"

Callie shook her head. "Not a chance. If we are going to pull this off, my uncle gave me a packet and some gold that I buried on the night he was taken away. Jacob thinks I'm dead. He would never suspect I have the deed to the ranch or the gold. I know he was trying to get both the gold and the deed. Right now the ranch is still in his name unless the state gave it to him since my uncle is in the asylum."

"I don't believe they have, according to my sources. Why do you have gold?" Sheriff Nightingale asked.

"My father and uncle both mined for gold in California before coming here. There was plenty left after we bought the ranch. Jacob, the lazy brother would not help to work the land, but he wanted to be partners."

"Most likely so he had a place to do his rustling, like he's doing now," Sheriff Nightingale quipped.

Callie stepped away from Samuel. "I have a plan. We should go to the ranch and retrieve the deed and gold first. There is also a signed document stating the ranch goes to me if anything happens to my Uncle Jessie. So as long as I can prove I am his niece and we are married, I doubt I'll have any problem getting Jacob out of there."

"Samuel, you will need to find a different wagon to begin your journey to the Lunatic Asylum, since our wagon was given to a Chinese family." Nora smiled at Callie, not in judgement but mirth. She continued, "You can hitch up the one I use to go to Cooper's Ridge every Sunday. It's lightweight and will get you there faster. The rest of the men can count the herd while you take care of business."

Ma was always good at directing everyone. Even the rangers and sheriffs allowed her to take charge instead of giving any orders. They seemed to be in agreement to what she said.

Callie turned to him. "I will need a shovel or two to take along."

Samuel frowned. "What? Do you plan to bury someone?" His remark had him smiling instead when he realized she needed the shovel to dig up her documents and gold.

She shook a finger at him. "You never know!"

"We better get started, there's a lot of work to do."

A half hour later the wagon was hitched and the two were on the bench, ready to ride towards the North Texas Lunatic Asylum with a secret stop at the Double J Ranch.

Samuel heard a commotion behind him. Nora White stood at the barn, her hands on her hips. She nodded to the riders coming towards the wagon. Luke and Adam rode up beside them.

"What's this?" Samuel noticed their saddle bags were filled.

Adam chanted at the same time as Luke. "Can't let you go alone, brother."

Samuel wasn't afraid to go alone but with his brothers by his side, he knew whatever happened at the Lunatic Asylum, if need be, they'd be able to get Mr. Johnson out. The three of them had a way of getting things done.

"Thanks, Luke. Adam." He nodded, turned to Callie, who was pleasantly surprised the other two were along for the ride.

"This is good," she told him. "If we have to break him out, it's better to have more men. Did you plan this?"

He shook his head. "It's what brothers do. No one faces things alone, not when we have each other for support."

Callie sighed. "I'm so glad. It's going to be somewhat scary to go on the Double J land but I buried the goods far enough away from the main house no one will ever notice us. At least, I hope not."

"We'll find out when we get there," Samuel told her. He fingered his pearl-handled pistol just to make sure it rested on his hip. Callie was his wife now, he had to protect her at all costs.

Chapter 4

Callie's heart raced as they trudged through the field. "I forgot how high the water gets sometimes. I hope it didn't wash anything away." She had planted the metal box under the giant oak tree that stood on the edge of the creek that ran along the edge of the Double J's property line. As far as she knew, the area wasn't good for grazing and it was a bit too rocky. It was why she had picked the area to hide the metal box.

"I can see why the cattle don't come down this way. We've been walking for what seems like hours and nothing but rocks and gravel here. It's actually a good choice to hide something, Callie." Samuel patted her on the shoulder. "You doing alright?"

"I'm fine. The sooner we get this and get off this land, I'll feel better. Jacob will shoot first and ask questions later. If he see's I'm alive, he will surely kill me."

"He's not going to find us," Luke reassured. "I'll stand guard right here. Adam is with the horses and wagon and will warn us if anyone gets close."

"Hand me the shovel," Callie told him.

The cold metal was cool against her hand. Samuel took the other shovel, following her to the base of the old oak tree. "It's pretty rocky right here," he mentioned.

"I know, I did this on purpose. No one would ever think to bury something in this mass of rocks and stones." She scooted to one end of the tree and began moving the tip of the shovel against the pile. Moss grew on the tree trunk in abundance since it was so close to the water's edge.

"Let me do the laboring," Samuel offered.

Callie looked up. He was so handsome as he worked diligently to shovel away the heavy stones. Taking his boot, he pushed the tip into the loose earth, bringing up lots of gravel and dirt. He scooped them onto a pile. "How far did you dig?"

"I'm not sure, maybe a foot." In her desperation to bury her uncle's things, she hadn't realized exactly how deep she went.

"I feel something." The tip of his shovel hit something hard. When he moved it away, Callie knelt and pushed away the dirt with her hands. It was late in the evening, almost dusk, rendering it harder to see.

"I got it," she said, pulling the metal box out. Samuel bent down beside her. They were practically cheek to cheek. He moved ever so slightly, his warm breath against her skin.

"You sure do," he told her.

Somehow she didn't think he meant the metal box.

Being so close to him felt nice but they would not be allowed to dally. "We have to close up the hole and get out of here." Callie held the metal box in her arms while Samuel filled the hole with the mound of dirt and stones.

"Let's go," he told her. As they made their way back to Luke and Adam, he noticed there was a tiny lock on the front. "Did you know the box has a lock there?"

"Yes," she said, a big smile on her face. "I have the key right here." She pulled a chain from around her neck. It revealed a small key hanging there.

"The key to the box, very smart indeed. I'd say, your uncle and you did a good job of concealing things from the lazy uncle. Except he was a bit smarter in placing Jessie in a lunatic asylum. We better get moving."

They rode most of the day, Callie holding the metal box as if there was buried treasure inside. In all reality, it was everything she needed to exonerate Uncle Jessie and get him out of the asylum.

She was glad when one of the brothers announced they would be stopping for the night.

"We asked Sheriff Montana to send a telegram ahead to the hotel to hold two rooms for the night. This way we can start out early in the morning. We'll have a good nights rest this way. We have to be ready for anything."

Callie was surprised everything was already mapped out. She was used to dealing with things of this nature on her own. She turned to him. "Thank you. It's been a long time since I've had someone look out for me."

Samuel patted her hand and gazed into her eyes. "You don't have to worry any longer. That's my job now."

Tears sprang to her eyes. She tried to brush them away without him seeing them but it was too late. He closed in, taking a finger and wiping it from her cheek.

"I'm sorry, I don't cry. I never do."

He smiled and yet his eyes gazed into hers, so serious she sucked in a deep breath. It was almost dark but she was able to see every single feature of his face. The man was so handsome and yet his intense look made Callie feel safe.

Adam rode up alongside the wagon, making enough noise to wake the dead. "We're almost here. Take a left at the next crossroads and the hotel is on the left. I'm sure you remember that place."

Samuel nodded, then turned towards the road ahead, paying attention to the other wagons coming their way. She watched his profile for the longest time, remembering the kiss at their wedding ceremony, wondering when he was going to kiss her again.

They dropped off the horses and wagon and walked up the street to the main hotel. It was a large, elegant structure. She wasn't used to such luxury and she wondered how they acquired a room here. "Isn't this expensive?" she asked, worried about the cost. Even though she held a metal box full of gold if they needed money, she was always frugal. It was how they ran the ranch.

"No worries," Adam told her. "We have some history at this hotel. It's quite the story. Perhaps Samuel will let you in on his shenanigans at some point."

"My shenanigans? Why, you and Luke were up to your elbows in it, too!"

The three men laughed out loud. Callie found them refreshing in light of the heavy turmoil approaching. She had been so worried about her uncle, this reprieve from the seriousness of the day was well received.

"I wish to hear about the White brother's shenanigans," she told them.

"Let's get checked in and we'll tell you the story at supper." Samuel got two keys from the desk. They walked up a large open stairway to the first floor. As Luke and Adam went in one room, Callie realized she'd be sharing a room with her husband.

A nervousness overcame her senses. "Are we staying in the same room?"

"We *are* married." He unlocked the door and flung it open. A large bed stood right in her line of vision.

Callie gasped. How in the world would she be able to sleep in that bed with him? She turned to stare at his face, wondering what he was thinking. "You can't be serious? Is the other room just like this one?"

"I'm not sure, I suppose so."

She turned towards the bed. "I, do you think we should be doing this?"

"Callie, stop. We are married. It's perfectly normal for a married couple to sleep in the same hotel room."

"In the same bed?"

He laughed. "Yes, in the same bed. Where is your spirit, Callie? I'm surprised you are being so nervous about our situation."

Red flooded her cheeks. They felt warm. "I, uh, oh dear!" She didn't know what to say or do.

He came closer. She backed up. "Callie, what has gotten into you?"

Her lower lip quivered. "It's just, well, when I was young, we lived in a mining camp. I remember some of the married couples, they would, you know, um, do things in the tents right next to ours and I remember holding my hands over my ears because, well, there was a lot of noise and growling."

He gathered her in his arms. Was he chuckling? He didn't scare her, far from it but the memory of her younger years came flooding back. Callie even surprised herself at the intensity of her memory. Some of the men were not nice to their wives. She remembered her father cursing at some of the miners and he always tried to pitch their own tent away from others after that incident but it remained in her head all these years.

Callie hadn't realized how much until she saw the bed and her husband in the same room together. "I'm so sorry, Samuel. I had a bad memory and it gave me the chills."

He looked down at her. "I'll go stay in my brothers room so there is no need to worry."

She looked up at him. "Are you certain?"

"Are you?"

She nodded. "It would be for the best."

He bent down and kissed her softly on the mouth. "I promise, whatever bad memories you had I vow right now to replace them with unforgettable ones. This is my promise to you."

Then he was gone.

She stood in the center of the room, staring at the door he just closed. What a wonderful, caring man. He was her husband and had every right to be here and yet he went next door in a crowded room on her behalf. Was he sleeping on the floor? A chair? She didn't know but his tender arms that held her while she was scared made her re-think everything she knew about men.

Would he be gentle with her?

That is, if she ever had the chance for a real marriage with him.

They were together for two reasons. He married to honor a promise to his Ma and she needed him to get Uncle Jessie out of that horrible place. She shuddered at the thought of having to face the doctor again. He had been so awful to deal with.

Except this time she wouldn't be alone. She had her new husband along to speed up the process. Dr. Wallace did say if she were married, he'd be inclined to allow Uncle Jessie to leave in her husband's care. And if that didn't work, she had another plan to break him out. All she had to do was put it in motion.

After a pleasant dinner in the hotel's dining room, she retired to her room, crawling under the covers in a daze. It had been a long day, well, a long week.

She stared at the ceiling for the longest time. *Dear Lord, please be with us tomorrow. Keep Uncle Jessie safe from those madmen at the lunatic asylum and help me get him home. Amen.*

The road she was on would always be rocky. Without a mother, life had always been somewhat harsh. She grew up in the presence of her father and uncle, living a rough life as a miner's daughter first, then a rancher's daughter. She didn't dally when life got easier, no, she worked the ranch right alongside the rest of them. Even though she knew how to take care of herself, Callie was tired. It had been nice today when everything had been taken care of.

When Samuel's Ma took her in her arms and gave her a hug before they left the ranch, it felt so nice. There was something about an older woman giving a well meaning hug. She never knew her mother. Samuel was so lucky to have her. She drifted off to sleep wondering what it would be like to have Nora White as her mother in law.

<> <>

North of the tracks of the Texas and Pacific railway, a few miles North-east of the town of Terrell, stood an intimidating structure most people were afraid to get near in case one of the patients got loose.

The four of them stood at the gate, the sign glaring at them in bold letters. *North Texas Lunatic Asylum - for the treatment and care of the chronic incurable insane.*

Callie felt Samuels hand on her arm as she took a deep breath. "I guess it's now or never," she said, then turned to him with a nervous look. Letting out her breath, she took the first step forward. Samuel encased her hand in his, walking alongside of her.

"Did you get a chance to look through the box?"

Callie nodded. "I did so this morning. The deed to the property is there, along with a last will and testament leaving the ranch to me. There is also plenty of gold I will use to reimburse you and your family as soon as this task is over."

Samuel squeezed her hand. "No need, Callie. I have our wedding certificate right in my pocket, signed by the Reverend Conners. It is a bit crinkled." He pulled it out to show her.

Callie lifted her face to him. She smiled and then laughed out loud, even though the nervous energy filled her up. "You snatched up that piece of paper and stuffed it in your pocket right before we left the church."

"I did. Although I wish I remembered more about the ride back to the ranch."

She patted his arm with her other hand. "No need. We had an adventure, that's for sure."

He stopped at the front door, its intimidating size looming over them. "Are you ready?"

Callie nodded. "I think so. I want Uncle Jessie home."

He turned to his brothers. "If this doesn't work, let's go with the plan we came up with last night."

Callie looked surprised. "What plan?"

"I'll tell you after the meeting with Dr. Wallace if we are not successful. We better get on inside."

After ringing the bell, a large man in a white shirt opened up. The door opened in slow motion. Callie looked at Samuel, knowing it wasn't as unpleasant inside since everything was relatively new.

The large, open foyer led to several wings. Construction was everywhere, causing some interference with everyday functions.

"Don't mind the mess," an orderly told them. "How may I help you today?"

Callie spoke up. "We are here to see Dr. Wallace." She rocked up and down on her toes and heels, the excitement of freeing her uncle foremost on her mind.

"I'm afraid that is impossible. Did you have an appointment?"

Callie's lungs closed. She coughed. "An appointment? No. We have come to take my uncle home."

"I'm afraid that is impossible, also."

Fear engulfed Callie. She was prepared for a battle but this was awful. How rude not to even be allowed a visit with Dr. Wallace. "Sir, I am the niece of Mr. Jessie Johnson and I insist on speaking to his physician about his release."

The orderly shrugged. "Sure. But Dr. Wallace is gone."

"Gone? I beg your pardon!"

"He took a leave to settle some of his affairs in Austin. He won't be back for another month."

"Then, I'll speak with the next person in charge."

"Fine. That would be Dr. Wartling." He leaned over, his voice quiet. "I'll warn you now, he is nothing like Dr. Wallace."

Callie shifted her feet. "Well, then, let's go find him."

They followed the orderly down a long hall. A sign with the doctor's name was pasted to the wall on a small plaque. The door they stood in front of was ajar.

The orderly knocked and entered at the bark of a man with a loud voice. "Enter."

After several moments, Callie was about to burst into the room when the door opened wider and the orderly waved them in. "Thank you," she told him.

"Good morning." The doctor didn't stand up to greet them. He looked up from a pile of paperwork on his desk, frowning.

Since the doctor didn't offer a seat, she walked up to the desk, followed by the men. "Hello. I am the niece of one of your patients, Jessie Johnson. I'll get right to the point of the matter. This is my husband, Samuel White and his brothers, Adam and Luke. We are here to have Jessie Johnson released into our custody."

The doctor raised his head, tilting it to one side as if he were in deep thought. "That's impossible!"

"I beg your pardon? I understand you are taking the place of Dr. Wallace. I spoke to him a few weeks ago and he told me to bring my husband here to have Uncle Jessie released into our custody." The good doctor didn't exactly say it the way she told this man but close enough. She was determined her uncle was coming home today. Nothing could stop them.

Samuel moved to the desk and handed Dr. Wartling the crumpled sheet of paper, showing their proof of marriage.

He scrutinized the paper then handed it back. "I see. That's all well and good, except Mr. Johnson is no longer here."

Callie's throat tightened. She was told the only other way patients left here was when they died. She stumbled when her knees weakened but Samuel placed an arm around her waist, holding her up. "What do you mean he isn't here?" Her words came out in a hoarse whisper.

The look on the doctor's face appeared as if he were enjoying the conversation. Almost as if he wanted Callie to be upset. How could he behave this way? The man stood up. "Don't worry, he isn't dead if that's what you were thinking. It's an unusual case, I will say. Normally we bring the patients from the poor farm here to live out there days but Mr. Johnson didn't seem as fragile as the rest. As a matter of fact, he insisted on wanting to work and keep busy."

"If he isn't here, sir, where is my uncle?"

"Callie, let him explain." Samuel's soothing voice didn't help this time. She was clearly agitated and nothing Samuel or anyone else said to calm her would help until she knew where he was.

"Mrs.White, your uncle was sent to the Kaufman Poor Farm just yesterday. He is to live out his days working the farm to pay his way."

Callie pursed her lips. "He doesn't have to pay his way on a poor farm! He has a working ranch where he can live out his days."

Dr. Wartling looked confused. "According to the brother, Mr. Johnson signed it over to him."

Callie turned. She nodded to Luke who held the metal box. "May I?" She dished through the papers inside, placing the deed to her uncle's ranch in the doctor's hand. "Here is the proof to exonerate my uncle. There was no exchange, no signing over of properties. As a matter of fact, I am listed as his next of kin. The second document entitles me to the ranch, not Jacob." She didn't bother to explain the part where she was supposed to be dead.

The doctor read the documents and handed them back. "Everything seems to be in order but how do I know you didn't falsify these papers for your own good seeing as you have something to gain in this case?"

Samuel came to her rescue. He leaned over the desk and looked the doctor in the eye. "You don't, Dr. Wartling. But, I will tell you what is happening right now as we speak. The Texas Rangers have Jacob Johnson under investigation right now. There will be an arrest made within the next week. I suggest you write a letter to have Mr. Johnson released from the poor farm so your name does not become involved with this investigation."

The doctor nodded. He dipped his pen in the ink and scratched a letter on the available stationary on his desk. Fanning the paper to let the ink dry, he held it out for Callie. "Here is your letter. I do not want to see you here ever again."

Callie took the letter, turned and marched out of the room, not even saying good bye. The others followed, no one saying a word until they got to the front door. "Sir, if I may have a word with you?" Callie addressed the orderly who let them in.

"Yes, ma'am, how may I be of service once again?"

"Where is the Kaufman Poor House?"

He smiled. "It's around about a mile and a half from the courthouse square."

"If I knew where the square was, it would be more helpful." Callie gave the orderly one of her gorgeous smiles. He blushed and offered directions.

As they walked out of the intimidating building, Samuel and his brothers began to laugh. "You are a charmer, Miss Callie," Adam told her.

"Yes, sir, that smile you gave him made him blush." Luke poked Samuel in the ribs. "You better watch out for her, she'll have you eating right out of her hands."

"Stop it, the both of you. You are embarrassing Callie."

Callie laughed out loud. "Hardly, but thank you boys for the compliments. Now, he said to take a left first then go about a mile and a half so we best be on our way."

The began in the direction they were told while Callie's heart pumped erratically. She began to sweat profusely, dabbing her forehead with a handkerchief she pulled from the pocket of her blue jeans. She had worn the pants and same shirt she met Samuel in just in case they had to break out her uncle. It looked like that wouldn't have to happen now.

"It won't be long, Callie. Your uncle will be free and then what?"

She looked over at Samuel. He held the reins in his strong, muscular hands. Hands that worked his ranch day in and day out. She'd love to spend her entire life with him but now that her uncle was about to be free, she needed to be with him, to make sure he was always kept safe.

Although if her uncle knew she was falling for the man next to her, he'd be the first to tell her to follow her dreams. That was the type of man he was. Uncle Jessie lived life to the fullest. She smiled to herself. He was even making his stay at the asylum interesting, insisting they have him work for his room and board.

"I'm not sure what's next, Samuel. It's all so scary right now. I don't believe we can go back to the ranch yet, not until the rangers arrest Jacob."

"You and your uncle will come to the White Ranch for now and we'll work out the details later."

"Thank you, Samuel. Without you, I would have had to go to extremes to get Uncle Jessie out. What man is willing to help me like this? No one, except you." She nudged him with her elbow. "You are a great man."

Samuel grinned. "Well, you aren't so bad yourself."

They rode in silence the rest of the way. Callie wondered what a normal life with Samuel would be like before she remembered after the three months were up, she was going to go back to her uncle's ranch. Most likely alone.

How was she able to fall in love with Samuel so quickly? If it was love. Maybe she was feeling grateful for his help with her uncle. Yes, that's it, she was grateful.

Then why was her heart pounding like a runaway train every single time she looked his way?

Chapter 5

Samuel wanted the best for Callie. Since when did he get all touchy, feely about a woman? His original plans were to annul the marriage after three months. How was it he was starting to think otherwise? His feelings were getting in the way.

How in the world was he going to stay married to this woman for three months without any emotions if he was heading down that path in just a few short days?

Samuel looked at his two brothers, one on each side of the wagon as it made its way down the country road. Acres upon acres of farmland surrounded them even though the sign a mile back indicated the Poor Farm was in this direction.

His thoughts went to his brothers. Luke and Adam seemed happy with their wives. Adam had Melody, a lifelong friend and Luke, well, he fell head over heels in love with Abigail and now they were going to have a baby.

Life had changed for them all. Was he willing to break his promise to himself in order to keep Callie close?

They passed a grove of Cedar Elms and a Mulberry Mott as the structures began to appear out of nowhere. A large two story shabby house stood out among the other structures scattered over acres and acres of land. Samuel slowed the wagon.

Without a sign it was hard to tell if this was the place. He turned towards the home with a rusty looking roof. "I'll go check to see if this is the Poor Farm."

Callie slid from the wagon before he reached the ground. "I'm going with you."

His brothers stayed behind, alert, watching their surroundings. "I'll be right back, keep your eyes open," he told them, nodding to the men out in a field close by. It looked as if they were working the fields. He noticed some of the men staring at Callie, causing a wave of jealousy to overtake him.

Callie held the metal box in her hands. "I'm so excited to see my Uncle Jessie. It's been so long."

Samuel deliberately hooked his arm in hers, turning to the men in the fields for a long look. Some of the men turned away, understanding Samuel just laid claim to her. Others ignored his gesture, staring blatantly at her anyway. He almost stumbled over the step up to the wooden slab in front of the main door.

"We're in the right place, it says, Farm Superintendent House on this sign." Callie knocked before turning to look at Samuel with those beautiful eyes. They were filled with liquid, ready to pool over.

"It's going to be fine, Callie."

She smiled through her unshed tears. "I know, I'm so excited. Thanks for being here."

After several knocks, the door was flung open by a short, round man who barked out, "What is it?"

Samuel took over, not wanting Callie to deal with the man. He looked as if he hadn't washed in some time. Food dribbled from his chin. "Are you the Farm Superintendent?"

"Yeah, that's for sure. What happened now?"

He made no effort to allow them inside.

Callie spoke up. "Mr. Superintendent, I have some documents here that will be proof so my uncle may be released from this farm."

Callie was being kind calling this a farm. It looked more like a prison. He didn't draw attention to the one building they passed, which looked as if it had some bars on the windows. The more he thought about things, Samuel realized this was probably a place where they kept prisoners, as well as indigents from the war.

Rumor had it no one ever left here.

He hoped in her uncle's case they were wrong but they had a plan in case things got difficult.

"Is that a fact? What you got there in the box?" He stared at it, the greed oozing from his facial expression.

"That's none of your business until you tell me if Mr. Jessie Johnson is in your care?"

The man's face got beet red. It appeared no one ever talked up to him before.

Callie straightened her shoulders. "Mr. Superintendent, sir, I have a document here from Doctor Wartling of the North Texas Lunatic Asylum to release my uncle immediately if not sooner!"

His hand went to his hip. "Let me see."

"I'll be happy to oblige." Callie turned her back to the man, opened the box and locked it again. She didn't want him to see the gold inside. She was smart as well as sassy.

Turning back to the farm manager, Callie handed him Dr. Wartling's letter.

He wiped the food from his chin and stared at it. Then he took the letter, crumbling it up and dropping it to the ground.

Callie cried out.

Samuel took a step closer.

The man took a step backwards. "I got me a rifle right inside the door so no funny business. Now you be on your way."

Samuel propped his foot in the door jam. There was no way they were this close to be turned away. "She showed you the proof, now we will collect her uncle and be on our way."

The plump superintendent spat on the floor. "I ain't seen no proof. Besides, can't read. It don't matter none anyway, Johnson isn't here any longer."

"What?" Callie cried out. "Not again! Where is my uncle!" Her voice sounded so desperate Samuel wanted to hold her in his arms and tell her everything will be okay. But, he didn't know if it would be or not.

"Mister, I am not a patient man. Now, where is her uncle?"

The man grunted. "He took off, slid right out from under the watchman and fled. Yesterday evening. Stole one of our horses, too. Left an old pocket watch in exchange for the horse, so I ain't gonna have him arrested for stealing since the watch looks more valuable. You happy now! Now, go on, get off this property."

He slammed the door shut. Callie turned and knocked on the door before Samuel was able to stop her.

The door flew open. "Didn't I say to get on out of here!"

"I have something more valuable to trade for the pocket watch."

"What?"

"Gold."

The scruffy man stared at Callie. "How'd you get gold?"

"None of your business. I'll take a look at the pocket watch first."

He slammed the door. The moment he did Callie opened her metal box, taking out a small pouch. Samuel knew it was worth a small fortune. She had separated the gold, placing them in several small pouches inside the box.

A few minutes later, he opened the door and stepped outside. Callie stuck her empty hand out. "Let me see?"

He complied. She opened the watch, staring at the inscription on the inside. Samuel was concerned she'd fall apart when he saw the look on her face. The watch was important. Yet, instead of falling apart, she threw the little pouch to him.

The superintendent opened it up, grunted and went back inside.

Callie grinned. "Let's get out of here."

Samuel wrapped an arm around her shoulders as they made their way back to the wagon and helped her onto the seat. He gave the men in the field one more blatant look before riding away from the Poor Farm.

"I know where my uncle is going?"

At the end of the road, Samuel stopped so his brothers could catch up.

"What now?" Luke asked.

Callie had tears streaming down her face as she faced them. "I'm afraid we have to get to the Double J. He's most likely on his way there to confront Jacob."

"I wasn't expecting things to go like this," Samuel told her. "I figured we'd find your uncle without any issues. His escaping wasn't in the plans. We need to contact the rangers and have them get to your ranch before your uncle does."

Callie agreed. "We can probably get there sooner though. It's only about two hours from here."

"Well, then, let's get moving!"

Luke rode alongside the wagon. "It's be best if we get rid of the wagon."

Samuel nodded. "I think Ma is going to have our hide. This will be the second wagon we left behind." He drove into a grove of trees, unhitching the horse.

Adam and Luke helped while Callie stood on the sideline opening and closing the pocket watch.

Luke agreed. "We can come back for it later. If it's even here. Let's hide it further into the grove so no one from the road can see the wagon."

After making sure it was well hidden, Samuel helped Callie onto the horses back. "Have you ever been on a horse without a saddle?"

Callie nodded. "Yes, plenty of times." She flipped the pocket watch shut and placed it inside her metal box. "Adam, would you mind putting my belongings in your saddlebags?"

Since their horse had none, Adam placed her metal box in his saddlebag, tightening the rawhide to make sure it was secure.

"Let's ride for the ranch," Samuel yelled. They began a fast trot before breaking into a run. They'd go as far and as fast as possible until it was time to rest the horses.

Samuel was determined to protect Callie at all costs. She was determined to ride hell bent for leather into the ranch and save the day. He had to convince her otherwise.

Men were evil. They caused ill will and had wrong intentions. She was naive in that department and he needed to make sure nothing happened to her.

At all cost.

He wanted to keep Callie around for a long, long time.

His brother Adam looked over at him just as he realized how much he cared for Callie.

"Uh oh," he heard Adam say to Luke.

Luke watched him with guarded eyes. Then he nodded to his younger brother. "Yep, looks as if," but didn't finish the sentence.

Samuel kicked in his heels. He felt Callie's hands grip his waist as he raced down the road away from them, daring his brothers to keep up. This was one thing they were all good at, and he was in a silent race to cross over the finish line.

<> <>

Callie hung on for dear life. She almost lost her hat at one point but knew the brothers were all racing each other. A shout from her mouth came out almost before she realized. This was fun. Samuel was fun.

Even though she was scared out of her mind, Samuel was trying to distract her. She knew the odds were against Uncle Jessie if he got to the ranch before the rangers did. The only good thing was the fact the Double J was being investigated. Did that mean someone was already there, maybe undercover? If so, perhaps Uncle Jessie would be safe. Still, she couldn't help but worry about his safety.

As they went flying down the road, she clung onto Samuel's waist. His muscles tightened as he leaned forward, trying to beat his brothers to the next town. Callie laid her head against his back, laughing out loud, urging him on because she was rooting for Samuel to win, even if they weren't racing for any one thing.

The three riders made it to the town of Terrell in no time flat. The horses were winded so they let them rest and feed at the local livery. Callie found a small café down the street where they had a small meal.

"We've got to keep going," she told them, wiping her mouth with a cloth napkin. "Do you think the horses will be rested up by now? I am so nervous for Uncle Jessie?"

"We sent a telegram to Wichita Falls where Sheriff Montana will get it to the rangers. If he can't find them, he'll go himself. Don't worry, Callie, your uncle won't be alone."

Callie shuddered, even though she knew he was right. "He's had a good head start."

"He left late last night so he had to hunker down somewhere. Even if he headed out at daylight, he's not that far ahead of us."

Callie felt Samuel's hand over hers. It was warm and comfortable. She basked in this new feeling. No one had ever taken the time to make her feel as if everything was taken care of.

"On an older, weaker, worn out horse, I may add," Luke mentioned.

"What makes you think it's an older horse?"

Luke threw some bills on the table as he scooted back the wooden chair. "From what I saw the horses at the Poor Farm were not in tip-top shape. Your uncle will have to rest the horse more often than not. If we are lucky, we may get there the same time he does or before."

"I sure hope so." Callie was worried because she was sure Uncle Jessie left their without any money. He was a tough man but he was getting older. How would he get back to the ranch without food or water?

She fingered the little metal box in her lap. Callie simply refused to keep it in the saddlebags when they left the horses at the livery, even though there was a nice man overseeing everything. Still, she didn't trust anyone.

Samuel stared at her for a few moments. "Are you ready to hear the story of our adventure at the hotel in Dallas?"

"Yes, certainly."

Samuel and Adam took turns while Luke filled in some of the parts about Melody's ex-husband, who had divorced Melody but made her life so miserable she had been forced to leave town. Then, the three brothers came back and humiliated him in the hotel ballroom, in front of his partners and co-workers.

"It was hilarious and Samuel thought it up," Adam told her. "When the lady and her mother came through the door declaring he was the father of her baby, the whole room gasped."

Samuel grinned. "I bet he is long gone from Dallas."

Callie began to laugh, clutching at her belly. She almost doubled over.

"It was funny."

She laughed harder.

"Callie?" Samuel grinned.

Luke and Adam began to chuckle.

After a moment or two, everyone at the table was laughing, along with a few patrons of the next two tables.

Callie finally settled down. The brothers painted such a vivid picture of their experience it was almost as if she were there, too. "I think we better get out of here before they throw us out for misconduct."

They left the town of Terrell, heading towards the Double J Ranch. Callie hoped they would meet up with her uncle somewhere along the way.

<> <>

"We better stop and rest the horses."

Luke motioned to a grove of trees. The other riders followed until they were hidden from the main road.

"There is a small stream about fifty yards ahead," Callie told them. "Follow me." She led her horse to the small stream so they could drink up.

"How far?" Samuel asked.

"Ten minutes time we'll be on Double J land." Her voice shook. Adrenaline was rising at the thought of facing her lazy uncle. She wanted to shoot him for all the worry and ill-will he caused. She also wanted to see his face when she rode in there very much alive!

"What are you thinking about, Callie?"

Samuel was a good man. He seemed to care about her well being. He was also fun and he loved to laugh. She knew with him by her side she didn't have to fear her uncle. "I can't wait for him to see I'm not dead after all."

"He may try to shoot you so I want you to stay close to me. I'll protect you, Callie. I won't let anything happen to you."

She turned, placing a hand on his cheek. "Those are the sweetest words I've ever heard. Thank you, Samuel."

He dipped his head and placed a kiss on her mouth. Callie closed her eyes, revelling in his sweet kiss. If things went wrong and something happened, at least she'd have this wonderful kiss.

She was starting to feel different about Samuel. The more she spent time with him, her heart was leading to the fact she wanted to spend the rest of her life in his arms.

Was that a terrible thing? It was only if he asked her to give him an annulment after three months?

She didn't want to any more.

No, she was falling in love with Samuel.

The way he was looking at her right this very moment made her wonder if he wasn't feeling the same way.

"We best keep moving. Check your firearms, men." Luke liked to be in charge. The other brothers followed his lead, checking their guns before heading back down the road. Callie tucked her hair under her hat. She didn't want her uncle to know who she was until she was close enough to see his face.

It was going to be quite the reunion.

A few miles down the road, someone sat by the side of the road, holding their leg as if hurt. The person waved.

"Be careful," Luke told them, "it may be a trick. Be at the ready."

The others fingered their holsters, alert for any danger. Callie held on to Samuel as the horse trotted close to the stranger on the road.

Then she laughed out loud. "Uncle Jessie! Uncle Jessie! Samuel, it's my uncle! We found him!"

As soon as the horse came to a halt, she slid from the saddle, not waiting for Samuel to help. Kneeling down on the ground, she threw her arms around her uncle, who hugged her back.

"I'm so happy to see you are alive and well," Uncle Jessie said, holding her face in his hands. He got up from the ground, a little wobbly at first until he found his footing. "Who are your friends?"

"This is Samuel, and his two brothers, Luke and Adam. We are going to bring down Jacob. There are even Texas Rangers on the case. He's done some bad things since you've been taken away."

Jessie shook hands with the men. He swiped at the sweat dripping from his brow then pulled his hat down over his eyes to block the sun. "I'm much obliged. Jacob will pay for what he has caused." The look in her uncle's eyes didn't bode well with Callie. This was the first time in her life she was afraid for him.

"What do you plan on doing, Uncle Jessie?"

"I'm not sure yet. Mayhap I'll send him to the North Texas Lunatic Asylum."

"He'd sure deserve to go there," she told him. Her uncle looked thinner. He wasn't a tall man to begin with, but he was sturdy, and strong. Right now, he seemed weaker. His gray and black peppered beard was longer than usual. It didn't look as if he was taken very good care of in that place.

"What you got there?" Uncle Jessie asked Adam, pointing towards his mare. "I've got one exactly like her. As a matter of fact, she looks almost like my Mary Lou."

Her uncle began to walk to the mare, running a hand down her mane. He began to whisper to the mare while the others watched. Callie turned away to see Samuel watching her.

"You sure he's alright?" he asked.

Callie nodded. "He loves horses. Has a special love for them, even talks to them as if they are his own child. Don't worry, he'll be fine."

A shout riveted through the air as Callie turned to find her uncle riding like a madman away from them. The three brothers had been distracted, listening to her while her uncle stole their horse right out from under them.

"Uncle Jessie, you get back here! Don't try to go it alone!" She ran after, waving her arms but it was no use.

She turned to the others.

Adam was already mounted with Luke behind him. Samuel helped Callie up and they began the race for time to catch up with her uncle.

"What made him ride off like that?" Samuel shouted to her.

"He is madder than a hornet's nest, I'll tell you that. I would be too after what Jacob did but Uncle Jessie is in no shape to go after him alone. I'm so worried."

Samuel nodded. "What do you suppose he'll do?"

"He will ride in there like a warrior and make Jacob face him, one on one. I'm so scared for him!"

Samuel called to the others. "We better hurry."

They rode as fast and hard as their horses would allow, not stopping until they saw the sign for the Double J Ranch.

s

h

Chapter 6

The riders followed the dust from Uncle Jessie's trail. He hadn't gone in through the main road after all.

"I know where he is going," Callie shouted. "Follow the trail to the right." She pointed to a small break in the road, where a worn down trail covered in dry grass led into a small grove of trees. "This will take us almost to the main house. I forgot all about this one. My Uncle Jessie is brilliant."

"How so?"

"It will take us right behind the main house. There is a batch of mulberry trees about a foot from the pantry door. I'd say they are about twenty five feet high so no one will know we are coming. Uncle Jessie does have his senses about him. I was getting worried when I saw how frail he looked."

"Frail body doesn't mean the mind is too," Samuel told her. "Let's not talk, we don't want to give ourselves away. I see the house roof up ahead."

They tied the horses to the first mulberry tree, careful to keep them far enough away so no one heard them coming. The three brothers followed the path through the grove, treading as lightly as possible. Samuel had asked her to wait with the horses but when he saw her face, he clammed up and let her come along. There was no way she was staying behind.

He walked ahead of her, claiming if someone sees them and shoots, he'd get hit instead of her. She almost teared up at the thought of him taking a bullet for her. Did that mean he truly cared? Enough not to annul the marriage in three months?

Callie crossed her fingers and giggled.

"What's so funny?" Samuel turned his head slightly and whispered.

"Oh, nothing. Was thinking about something wonderful."

"We're almost at the door. Keep quiet or you stay outside."

"You bossing me around, Samuel?" She was teasing. He looked way too serious.

"You bet I am. Here we go. Callie, are you sure you want to come inside?"

"Yes. I want to see his face when-"

Adam opened the back door to hear voices coming from somewhere inside. Jacob was ranting at the cook to hurry up with his lunch before stomping out of the kitchen.

They carefully made their way inside, crowding into the back room that led through to the large open sitting room. Instead of going that way, Callie followed the hallway towards the kitchen, by-passing a large, round woman with an apron. She held a finger to her mouth.

The woman nodded and stepped back, allowing them to pass through.

As they came around the corner, Callie stopped suddenly when she looked out the large window to see the familiar faces of the two rangers walking up the path to the front door. She held up her hand and pointed. Samuel by-passed her and took the lead. He glared at her, probably because she went ahead of him. Men were so strange.

Callie had taken the lead because she knew the house better than any of them. She wasn't about to jump out and confront her uncle without a plan of action. Not just yet.

Then he stood there, his back to her as he answered the front door. Callie's legs moved forward until she felt a hand on her shoulder. She hung onto the metal box still in her possession.

"We'd like to ask you a few questions, Mr. Johnson." Noah Calloway flashed a badge.

"What can I do for you gentleman? I'd invite you in but I need to get to the south end of the ranch to take care of an issue down there."

"No need. We've already taken care of that issue," Grant Jennings told him.

"What do you mean?" Jacob asked. His voice wasn't quite as strong and confident as it was a few moments earlier when he yelled at the cook. Jacob ruffled a hand through coarse gray hair.

Callie stood at the doorway closest to them, peeking her head around the corner. Samuel was so close his warm breath fluttered across her cheek. When she turned to give him a worried look he placed a small, quick kiss on her mouth.

How was he able to be so frisky and kiss her at a time like this? As Callie gazed into his eyes, she noticed an intensity that burned for her. She knew right then and there he was in love with her.

Callie sighed. She loved him as well but needed to see this through. As her feet moved forward, Samuel realized what she was going to do. He reached out to grab her arm but she dodged his hand.

Her voice drowned out the others. "Hello, Jacob."

He swung around, away from the front door where he had been talking to the rangers, which allowed them to step inside. His jaw dropped when she lifted her hat to let layers of hair fall across her shoulders and down her back.

"You are dead!" His eyes widened in disbelief.

"I'm very much alive."

"Fooled ya, you dirty, low-down rotten scoundrel!" Uncle Jessie came out of nowhere, holding a Winchester rifle. He leveled it at his brother's chest.

Jacob Johnson was caged in like a tiger in a circus cage. "How'd you get out of the lunatic asylum?" Callie watched as he tried to talk to distract his brother. She looked down to see his cowboy boots sliding discreetly backwards, inch by inch. The movement was so slight, no one would take notice unless they were staring at his boots like Callie was doing.

There was a small desk against the wall he was inching his way towards. Callie bet a loaded gun was on the shelf and there was no way he was going to foil anyone ever again!

She moved so fast Samuel didn't have a chance to hold her back. Callie marched towards her uncle, passing by him to stop at the small secretary in the corner of the room. Low and behold, a pistol was tucked in the back underneath a shelf.

As she reached out to grab the gun, her uncle swung away from the others and pushed her away. She fell against the wall.

Hard.

His quick movement took her by complete surprise but she shot back at him, taking the metal box in her hand and bringing it down over the back of his head.

Jacob stiffened for a brief moment before turning to her with the gun in his hand.

Metal slid from leather as each man pointed their gun at Jacob.

"I wouldn't try anything stupid," one of the rangers told him.

"You may shoot me but this one is supposed to be dead. Perhaps we should make that happen."

"Over my dead body," Uncle Jessie pointed the rifle higher.

"No! Over mine." Samuel lunged at Jacob before anyone had a chance to get a shot off.

Callie screamed.

A shot rang out.

She watched the man she loved in horror. He stilled. His eyes were hard and intense.

Then he pushed himself away from Jacob as the body lost its footing and fell to the floor.

Jessie stepped closer. He aimed the tip of the rifle and kept it on Jacob. He cocked the lever. "You ain't dead yet? Don't you move!"

Jacob bled from his shoulder but he was very much alive. He looked up at Jessie with fear and loathing. "Don't shoot me, please," he begged. "I'm sorry! I just wanted a piece of the ranch, I didn't mean what I did."

"You coward!" Jessie kept nudging the Winchester closer.

Callie was afraid he'd shoot Jacob dead. "Uncle Jessie, don't kill him. He needs to have a taste of what you went through. As his kin perhaps you can suggest he spend some time in a lunatic asylum!" She didn't want him to get arrested for killing Jacob in front of two Texas Rangers.

Jessie spit on the floor near his brother's side. "I'm a forgiving man, Jacob, and you know this. Except not this time. You fooled us all. There's no forgetting what you did. What goes around, comes around and you are about to feel the long arm of the law." He nodded to the rangers. "Get him out of my house!"

"It ain't your house no more!" Jacob groaned when the two rangers picked him up by the arms. He cried out, blood dripping from his wound.

Callie stepped forward. "I've got the deed right here. Shows what you know, Jacob. This metal box was buried right here on the Double J, right under your nose!"

"I'll get you back for this!" Jacob screamed as they took him away. Several other law men outside were rounding up some of his co-horts.

"I want every man who associated with him gone." Uncle Jess leaned back, wiping sweat from his forehead.

Callie put her arms around him. "I'm so happy to know you are safe at last."

He held her for the longest time. Samuel and his brothers stepped outside to help the law men while they made their way to the kitchen.

She looked at her uncle. "I'm going to spend some time here with you, Uncle Jessie, but I want you to know something."

He nodded. "I think I already do. Does it have anything to do with the feller who jumped in front of me to save you?"

She smiled. "It sure does. He is my husband."

He shook his head. "I am not sure how that came about but we got all day, my girl! I want to hear about this from the moment I was forced into that lunatic asylum."

Callie put on a pot of coffee. "Doris, can we get something to eat? My husband and his brothers must be starving by now."

She placed two plates filled with meat and potatoes on the table. "I'm way ahead of you, Callie, dear. Dig in. I'm so glad you both are back. It's been quite a mess here."

"Thank you, Doris. How have you faired?" Jessie was always so good to her. She was a widow of ten long years and Jessie gave her a job when her husband died on the trail.

"I'm fine. I'll go fetch the others."

Callie noticed as Doris turned to leave, she pinched Uncle Jessie's cheek. He took her hand and gave it a squeeze. Well, look at these two, she thought to herself. A romance was brewing right in front of her eyes.

Callie hadn't realized how pent up her emotions were. They all sat at the table, laughing, eating and talking about ranch stuff. A few times Callie chanced a look at Samuel but he was deep in a serious conversation with her uncle.

Jessie dropped his napkin on an empty plate and cleared his throat. He took a butter knife and tapped it on the tip of his water glass. The room got quiet fairly quick. "I just want to say to all of you, the White boys, the rangers involved and my darling niece Callie that this old codger appreciates every single thing you all did to try to save me."

Callie sat on his right. She leaned over to place a kiss on his cheek. "I would have done anything to make sure you came back home to where you belong. I love you Uncle Jessie."

He patted her hand. "I love you, too, my dear child. Now, it's time for an old man like me to go to bed. You are all welcome to bed down here and stay as long as you want."

After Uncle Jessie went off to his bed, Callie helped Doris clean up the dishes. The three brothers went outside with one of the ranch hands to take a look at the ranch. Callie was glad to have a few minutes alone.

She sighed. It had been a long few weeks faking her death, losing her uncle and even dressing as a boy. The thought occurred to her she didn't have to any longer.

"Why the frown, honey?" Doris took the pile of plates from her and set them in the soapy water.

"I kind of like my blue jeans," she said, her voice cracking. Wearing them led her to the life she was about to live now. With Samuel.

Doris grinned. "Well, who says you have to get rid of them. Why, your uncle bought five pair of them. You will have blue jeans coming out your ears."

Callie laughed. "Oh, Doris, I missed you so much." She gave the woman a hug. "I'm going to miss you even more now that I'm married and will be living at the White Ranch. Well, that's if I'm not sent back in three months."

Doris turned to her. "What kind of talk is this? A husband can send you back? I've never heard of such a thing!"

"Do you remember when all of this happened and I sent the letter to Miss Addie so I was able to become a mail order bride since I needed a husband fast?"

"I do. I thought it was a strange idea but you seemed to have pulled it off quite well and got yourself a fine man in the process."

Callie agreed. "There was a clause in the contract. If within three months the marriage bed wasn't fulfilled, either one of us were allowed to have the marriage annulled and the other one had to agree."

Doris whistled. "That's quite an arrangement. Let's see, you haven't used up much of the three months."

"No, it actually has been so fast I've hardly gotten to know him."

"Maybe you should wash your hands of the whole ordeal right now. Ask for an annulment now."

Callie hesitated. "I think he cares for me."

Doris turned to stare at Callie. "Do you feel the same way?"

She nodded. "I do."

Doris grinned. "Well, then, what's the problem? What are you doing in here washing dishes. Get on out there and tell your man how you feel."

Callie gave her another hug. "I love you, Doris. You and my uncle are perfect for each other."

Doris giggled in response. "I'm going to show him how much, too. After he gets a good nights rest because after that, he's not going to have much time to do so."

Callie covered her ears. "Oh, Doris, please! I don't want to know these things!" She laughed as she took off the apron and went outside to find Samuel.

There was some things they needed to talk about. Now was as good a time as any.

Chapter 7

Samuel noticed Callie the moment she came outside. He turned his head. Even wearing men's blue jeans and a wrinkled shirt, he thought she was beautiful. Her large hat covered most of her face but he knew what was under there. He knew the smile she always gave him, the creamy color of her skin and those eyes he wanted to gaze into and tell her how he never wanted to let her go.

"Hey," he called out, waving her over. They were talking to one of the horse trainers, Liam, who had Luke's attention. He had been standing there, thinking about Callie the whole time.

Now, here she was, walking towards him with the same determined demeanor, exactly like she had the day they first met.

"Hi, Samuel. Can we go somewhere to talk?"

He nodded, placing a hand in the small of her back. "Why don't we sit on the porch."

She shook her head. "No, it's too close. Would you mind walking a ways? There is a bench under the large tree over yonder. We can sit there."

He nodded, walking alongside her, enjoying their brief walk even if no words were exchanged.

Sitting on the bench, he looked out to see his two brothers in the corral with Liam. They were working with one of the horses. "This is a nice spot. Not too close, yet close enough to keep an eye on your surroundings."

Callie nodded. "Yes, it's my favorite spot. Just enough shade to sit here and read a book. It's not too often I get time to enjoy this space."

"What is it you want to discuss?" He was blunt and to the point. Which is a good thing because he had a feeling she was about to be.

"Our marriage."

"Yes, we are married, aren't we?" His smile made the corners of her mouth turn up. He loved to make her laugh because she seemed to enjoy life to the fullest. She would be a good wife for him.

"We are. I was wondering, Well, I know my lazy uncle has been caught and everything can get back to normal now, but, I was, well," she began to stumble over her words as if not knowing what to say next. It was unusual for Callie to behave this way.

He turned to her, took her face in both his hands. "Callie, I love you."

She gazed into his intense eyes. "You, you do? Yes, I see that you do."

"Callie, do you love me?"

She nodded. "Oh, yes, yes I do!" Callie flung her arms around his neck. "I really do."

Their kiss was sweet. He wasn't sure who kissed who but her mouth on his was perfect. As if there would never be a bad day again as long as he held her in his arms.

Until they heard shouting. They looked up to see his brothers shaking their hands in the air and clapping and hooting! Callie hid her face in his chest. "I, do you hear them?"

Samuel flung his fist in the air, shaking it at his brothers. Their laughter and shouts continued on for another moment before they got back to their business of horses once again.

Samuel reached for her hands, entwining their fingers and holding them against his chest. "Callie, are you prepared to spend a lifetime with me *and* my brothers? This is my life and my brothers and their wives are a big part of it, too."

She stared at him. Then flung back her head and laughed. Kissing him again, she shook her head. "Your brothers may be a bit on the wild side but I love that about you and your whole family. They're not afraid to have fun, to be real in front of each other. Plus, they jump in when there's trouble. You are the family I've longed for all of my life."

She snuggled against him.

"I'll always be here for you, Callie. No matter what."

She looked into his eyes. "I know you will and I feel the same way. My whole life it's been my father and my uncle and me. I haven't been around many women except for Doris for the last ten years." She looked down at her blue jeans. "You may have to put up with a pants wearing wife for some time."

"I'll take you and those blue jeans any time," he told her. "Callie, I don't want to annul this marriage in three months. Can we send a letter to Miss Addie right now?"

"Right now? Even before we've discussed our marriage and all it entails?"

He shrugged. "Nothing much to discuss. We'll live on the White Ranch and you can come visit your Uncle Jessie any time you see fit. How about we invite him to the White Ranch first? We'll do up a big celebration for family and friends, just like Ma did for Adam. That way he'll know you are in safe hands."

"Samuel?"

"Yes, love?"

Callie smiled. "I want to stay here with Uncle Jessie for a bit to catch up with him. Ease him into the fact I'll be living a few hours away. Do you mind?"

"Want me to stay with you?"

"I would love it but you need to get that letter written to Miss Addie and let your Ma know what is going on. She must be worried sick."

He agreed. "I'm sure she's unsettled right now not knowing how we made out. Okay, here's the deal. One week."

"One week? I only get a week with my uncle?"

"I can't bear to be away from you longer than one week," he told her, kissing the tip of her nose.

She smiled at him. Their marriage was going to be interesting to say the least. With her smiling at him like so, he wasn't sure how he'd ever get any ranch work done.

<><>

Samuel knew his brothers would abandon him the moment they got home. He was left to tell Ma the whole sordid deal while the other two hurried home to their wives.

He didn't mind though. Samuel often spent time sitting on the porch with her, listening to her talk about the old days when his Pa was still alive. Even though she spoke of him less and less these days, there were times when she did rehash the past and he was always willing to listen.

It was the one thing that worried him. The way she told tales of his Pa made the man look like this great, upstanding citizen, brave and gallant and filled with respect for his family. Maybe he was a hero in her eyes, but Samuel knew better.

It made him sad knowing what he did.

But, Ma must never find out. The three brothers had vowed to never reveal the secret to anyone. Not even Callie. It wasn't a chance any of them were willing to take. Everything his Ma knew about her life with her husband would be crushed if she knew the truth.

Samuel realized not telling Callie would not be a good start to their marriage but this was a secret he had promised to keep no matter what.

He needed to speak with Luke. As far as he knew, Luke never told Abigail. How did he keep it to himself without feeling guilty? They seemed to be happy in spite of the fact Luke was keeping something from her.

Would he be able to keep the secret from Callie?

"What's on your mind, son?" his mother's soft voice rose out of the cool, evening air.

He stared straight ahead, realizing he had been thinking too much about the secret for way too long. He turned to her. "Ma, I am in love with my wife."

She chuckled. "Congratulations. I was hoping to hear those very words from you."

Samuel began to push back and forth on the wooden rocker. "We will be separated for one week but I miss her already and it's not even one full day. She's a great woman, filled with laughter and adventure and that smile, it hurts my heart in a good way."

Samuel stared at his mother's profile as she stared over the land she had shared with her family for so many years. A tear rolled down her cheek. Through all the tough years they endured, he never saw her cry. Not even when her husband died. Back then, she stood tall and proud, determined to raise her boys with every ounce of bravery she was able to muster. Samuel had known she put on a good front.

And now, for the first time ever, she was showing her emotions. She seemed more reachable now, so normal.

When she turned to her youngest son, he saw the raw love for the family in her eyes. "I'm so proud of every one of you boys. All I have wanted these past few years is to see each of you happy and with someone who melted your heart. Now you have found out what I was talking about all along. You would make your Pa proud." She dished out a hanky from the sleeve of her dress to wipe the tears away.

Samuel loved his Ma, they each had a special bond with her. The thought of keeping Callie from learning the secret was pushed to the back of his mind for now. This was the reason why. He would never let anyone reveal the secret and ruin this woman's life. Not now, not ever. Even if it meant he had to hide this one thing from his wife. He didn't feel good about the whole lie but he knew to devastate his Ma would be his undoing. His brothers felt the same way, he was certain.

He still wanted to talk to Luke, to understand how he kept the truth from Abigail. How could a heart be so torn between a mother and son and a wife and husband?

<> <>

Callie had enjoyed the past week with her uncle. She turned to him while the wagon made it's way towards her new home. "Uncle Jessie?"

"Yes, my dear?"

"I'm happy for you as well."

Jessie stared. "What does this mean? I am the same as I've always been, a rancher doing his job, living and loving my property until the day I die."

She patted his arm. "But isn't it nice to have someone special in your life?"

Jessie glared. He pushed his hat back while holding the reins with one hand. "Spill it out, girl! What are you talking about?"

"I know you and Doris have a budding relationship going?" Callie laughed out loud at the look on his face.

"A what? Budding relationship? I don't even know what that means!" He raised his voice, his cheeks getting redder by the moment.

"Oh, come on now, Uncle Jessie. It's obvious the two of you care deeply for each other. Every time I turned around, she was touching your shoulder or you ran a hand down her cheek. Yes, don't act shocked! I am observant."

He bit his lower lip. "That you are! Well, then, I confess. Yes, I'm in love with Doris. I've even been thinking of asking for her hand."

Callie wasn't surprised, not one bit. She was so happy. This would make it even easier to live in her new home with Samuel. "Good for you, Uncle Jessie. You deserve every bit of happiness. Especially after what you been through at that asylum."

He had told her some of the stories from his short stay there. Since the building was fairly new, there were only around two hundred patients there but it had the capacity to reach much more. The institution had plans to add many more patients, mostly from the working poor farms all over the state. She was so glad he was no longer there.

Callie smiled to herself remembering their adventure. She was so anxious to see Samuel again. Boy, would he be surprised when she got there.

"What you smiling about, girl?"

"Seeing Samuel again. I can't wait."

"It won't be long now. Another hour and we'll be on White land. I'm anxious to see their ranch."

"Uncle Jessie, will you stay awhile?"

"Overnight, then I must get back home. I have a ranch to run. Jacob left me with a mess on my hands. I'm only leaving to make sure you get settled in. Besides," he grinned as he turned his head so she could see his eyes dancing, "I'm anxious to get back to my darling, too."

Callie giggled. She never thought she'd hear her uncle talk about love. It was nice.

She was so excited to get home. Home to Samuel. She shifted in her seat. It would be another hour until she saw him again. After a week, Callie had missed him so much she wasn't able to sleep last night.

That's when she had tip-toed across the living room to find her uncle and Doris on the front porch, holding hands like two young lovers. It was so adorable. Before seeing them like that, she had been worried her uncle would be alone and planned to travel back and forth to make sure he was well taken care of. Now, she didn't have to worry one bit.

Doris would see to him, she probably had been for the last few years, except Callie had been to busy to recognize the looks between the two of them. She hoped her and Samuel would develop a long-lasting relationship.

"Your new husband seems like a fine, upstanding citizen. But I'll say it again, Callie, if he treats you wrong, you high-tail it home and I'll take care of the rest."

Callie smiled at her uncle's overprotective words of wisdom. She patted his hand. "I'm sure I'll be fine. Samuel is one of the most trustworthy, honest and loyal men I've ever known. His brothers are the same way. I doubt they have a deceiving bone in their bodies."

Uncle Jessie rubbed a hand across his chin. "I've been around a long time, girl. Been lied to, beaten and in the days of mining gold, there was always someone trying to steal, cheat or lie. Not much has changed. Look at your own kin, Jacob."

She shrugged. "Jacob is a bad example. He was always a low-down, lazy man."

"Well, you may be right about that one. Yep, he is not a good example at all."

"I know what you are trying to tell me without telling me, Uncle Jessie. I love Samuel. He's a good man. I know there isn't any secrets there. He is one of the most honest men I know. I promise you won't have to worry."

"Well, I'm going to have a man to man talk with him just to be sure."

Callie rode the rest of the way contemplating Uncle Jessie's talk. He would let Samuel know in a kind of nice, threatening way not to hurt his niece. She already knew the tone of voice he'd use and was anxious for him to get it over with. There would be no talking her uncle out of the talk, so wasn't even going to try. She had better warn Samuel though.

The wagon turned down the lane at the sign with the bold letters that carved the name of the White Ranch. Callie shielded her eyes from the bright sun. In the distance the yard was set up almost exactly like she had remembered the day her and Samuel came riding in on the Chinaman's horse.

Had it been only a few short weeks? It seemed as if she had known Samuel forever. Her heart began to pound at the thought of seeing him.

Her excitement grew the further down the road they went. Then she was there, in front of the house, it's large two-story frame looming over head. The yard was filled with tables with food piled high. Neighbors, family and friends mingled everywhere.

Callie took a quick look around. She noticed his brothers, laughing with their wives while Nora spoke quietly with the old red-headed ranch hand Rusty.

The corral was empty so she looked to the barn, where some of the hands were mingling with their guests. Callie sat on the bench petrified. Where was her husband?

Was he even there? All this excitement brewing in her blood and now that she was here, she wasn't able to find him anywhere.

Uncle Jessie helped her down. "You go find your husband. I'm going to get me some food and introduce myself."

Callie smiled at her uncle. He wasn't one bit shy when it came to enjoying a reception. Nora had done this for her and Samuel. It was her gift to them, creating a beautiful wedding reception for the two of them.

Nora began to walk towards her when her Uncle Jessie held out his hand. The two shook hands and began to speak as Nora nodded to someone on the porch.

Callie looked over. Her husband stood here, frozen to the spot. His hands were deep in his pockets as he leaned back on his heels. The look of surprise on his face was overwhelming. What was wrong with him? He acted as if he were frozen and couldn't walk.

"Samuel! Hello?" She called out to him before making her way to the porch.

He shook himself, literally shook his head back and forth before he ran down the steps of the old wooden porch and picked her up in the air and spun her around so quickly she was stunned.

Then she flung back her head and laughed out loud.

There was some clapping going on behind them but Callie was not going to look because she knew it was his brothers. Once again they were being brothers. She was no longer embarrassed by anything they did.

Samuel stopped twirling her in circles. Her feet finally touched the ground. He gazed into her eyes with such an intense look that she gasped.

"I love you, Callie. I've missed you."

His lips brushed against hers in a sweet kiss. Her hands went to his face, she wanted to touch him, to know that he was real.

"I love you, Samuel White. I missed you right back."

"You sure do look beautiful. I think I like this side of you."

She blushed. "What do you ever mean? In a dress? Oh, Samuel, I may love my blue jeans but dressed up like this and the way you looked at me just now, well, I'll chuck the blue jeans if you act like this around me every day."

He nuzzled her neck and whispered in her ear. "I like the blue jeans, too. Don't get rid of them just yet."

She laughed at his brazenness.

Nora came up just then with Rusty and Uncle Jessie in tow. "Now that we've all met, I want to welcome you to your new home, dear Callie."

Nora gave her a hug. It felt so good, almost like having a mother of her own. "Thank you, Nora. I'm glad to be here."

"Well, good. We are so happy to have you. You'll have to stay with me for some time until we figure out living arrangements. I'm afraid with everything happening so fast, Samuel didn't get a chance to build a cabin for the two of you."

Callie laid a hand on her sleeve. "I'm quite fine with staying in the main house. As long as you don't mind."

Nora tilted her head. "Are you sure, dear? It's not a good start to a marriage living with your mother-in-law."

Callie gave Nora another hug, taking her by surprise. "I've never had a mother so it will be a pleasure living here with you."

"Thank you, but we will take it one step at a time. I will never impose on my children when it comes to their lives. For now, you are welcome to stay in the main house as long as you need."

Nora gave Callie a tour of the main house. Afterwards, they walked around the yard together while Samuel took her trunks and things up to their new room on the second floor. It wasn't long until Callie noticed Samuel on the porch looking for her. "There's Samuel. Thank you, Nora, I appreciate your kindness."

Nora gave her another hug. "You are welcome, dear. Now, if anyone asks, you don't know where I went. I must go unwind and rejuvenate. At my age it is harder to entertain these days."

Callie was surprised. "Has this been too much for you, Nora? I'm so sorry."

"No, dear. I haven't been sleeping and then worrying about the two of you has taken a toll. Most don't know how I worry. I never let anyone see when I get too tired. Here's the secret. Find a spot where you know no one will bother you for at least thirty minutes and bask in the silence."

Callie nodded. "I'm assuming you have a spot all picked out?"

Nora grinned. "I sure do. My horse loves my company and she's in the back of the barn so no one would suspect I go there to hide. I'll see you in a half hour."

Callie turned to find Samuel waving. She ran across the yard and took his hand. "Let's eat. I'm famished!"

They loaded their plates with food and sat down on a bench, laughing and talking with Luke, Abigail, Adam and Melody.

Melody was the first one to welcome Callie. "You've had quite the adventure. I've met your uncle, he is a very nice man."

Callie agreed. "Uncle Jessie is that and much more. I recently found out he has been having a romance with Doris, our cook."

Abigail jumped in the conversation. "The cook? Oh my! That sounds intriguing. Tell us the whole story from the beginning." She rubbed her growing belly.

As the three ladies talked while the men held their own conversation. Callie happened to overhear their conversation. She was having so much fun she didn't realize what was going on until she saw a stern look on Samuel's face.

"What are they doing here?" Samuel said to his brothers.

"Who?" Luke asked.

"Wesley and Russell Young and their mother."

"Not sure," Adam hesitated. "Maybe we should ask them to leave."

Luke held up a hand. "No, Ma invited them. She said it's time to let bygones be bygones. She said she wasn't even sure what all the fuss was about. After all these years, it was time to make amends."

Adam sighed. "It must have something to do with Samuel being the last of her boys to marry. This may be a problem. Let's go talk in the barn."

Samuel gave Callie a kiss on her cheek. "I'll be right back, love."

Callie gave him a worried look. "Is everything alright?"

He kissed the top of her head as he got up from the bench. "Perfect."

As the three men went towards the barn, Callie noticed the worried look on Melody's face. Abigail didn't seem to have noticed, she was still rubbing her belly. When Melody caught her staring, she turned away in a manner that led Callie to believe she was right.

She knew her husband. All was not well. There was something he was hiding. All three of the White men were hiding something.

And she had a hunch Melody knew what was going on.

<> <>

Samuel closed the barn door to keep the others out. Luke and Adam leaned against the first horse stall while he stood watch near the door. It was an unwritten code when the door was closed, it meant privacy. He hoped the other ranch hands would honor that right now.

"Okay Luke, what do you mean by your remark earlier?"

Luke crossed his arms. "Ma and I got to talking while you were out on the ranch this week. She wants us to try to get along with the Young family. Mrs. Young sent her a letter of apology some time back. It said that it's been ten long years since they haven't spoken and perhaps it was time to make amends."

Samuel swore. "I can't believe Ma would even consider befriending Mrs. Young after all this time. If Wesley and Russell get close and tell her the secret, her life will never be the same again."

Adam joined the conversation. "The Young's promised to never reveal who their father is. We've been paying them off for years. They are grown now, maybe it's time we stopped."

Luke lifted a hand. "Keep your voices down. Just because the door is closed, there are a lot of neighbors and members of the community out there. We don't want anyone hearing this conversation."

Samuel paced back and forth. He stood in front of Adam. "Don't make it sound like we are paying for their silence. Someone had to help Mrs. Young raise them after Pa died. She wanted to confront Ma if you remember."

Adam's eyes burned into his. "I remember that day plain as if it were yesterday. How she stomped across the yard ready to tell Ma she'd been having an affair with our father!" His voice shook.

"It wasn't an affair. Our father took advantage of her one time. When he realized what happened, he told me he tried to make it right but I'll never forgive him for cheating on Ma." Luke's determined low voice was louder than if he had shouted. It silenced the others. "When Mrs. Young's husband died, he swooped in there, trying to be kind and help her to take care of the farm, leaving us to do all the work here."

Adam nodded. "I remember well. Samuel, you were pretty young then, and may not have remembered. Ma took meals to the Youngs and sent Pa over to help her. They both tried to do their best by a neighbor but then Pa began to spend more and more time there, helping the widow out. Ma put a stop to it and even confronted the widow, which she denied. It was after that they never spoke again. Ma forbid Pa to help her any longer. Soon after that he was wounded by that wrangler and died."

Luke growled. "He's lucky he died that way. If Ma had found out, it would be much worse."

Samuel spoke up. "What are we doing here, brothers? Ma wants to make peace with Mrs.Young after all these years. If she gets too close to those boys she will know who the father is. Take a look at them, you can see who they look like. We can't allow this to happen. We've guarded his secret for way too long."

Luke turned. "He doesn't deserve it. If he weren't dead, I'd kill him myself. What do you two want to do about this situation? We can't let them get too close."

Samuel continued to pace. "I don't know. There's no solution.Wait! What if I started a fight with Wesley, he gets riled up fast and we all jump in with our wrestling moves. Ma won't put up with that and will throw them off the property."

Luke nodded. "It sounds like a reasonable plan. Something like that won't last forever, though." He took in a deep breath. "Sometimes I think we should out and tell her the truth but Ma is getting older. It may be too hard on her."

Samuel shook his head. "Why would we tell her after ten plus years of keeping the secret? Even after all these years it would kill her to know her husband and our father was a lying, cheating, rotten home wrecker!"

"Shh, Samuel, I hear the ladies. We better get out there."

"I'll put our plan into motion right away. No sense letting the Youngs get friendly with Ma. Where is she anyway?"

"Where's who?" Callie asked when he opened the door. The three brothers stepped out into the evening air.

"Ma." He looked around the yard, his eyes trying to adjust from inside the barn to outside. It was late afternoon but the day was starting to fade. It always did so much earlier this time of year. He placed his arm around Callie's shoulder as they began to walk towards the food tables where the Young brothers stood with the widow. "Are you having a good time?"

Callie smiled up at him, her face glowing. "I love your family and my two new sister-in-laws. I can't wait for Abigail to have the baby, plus this will be so much fun to have sisters close by. I missed out on siblings."

He gave her a sweet kiss on the cheek. "I can't wait to get you alone."

Callie flung her arms around his neck. "We can leave right now if you'd like Mr. White."

"I have something to finish with my brothers." He kissed the tip of her nose. "But afterwards, I'm all yours, Mrs. White."

"There she is."

He pulled her closer. "Who?"

"Your Ma. You asked where she was. She's standing right over there in the doorway to the barn. She said she was going to go visit with her mare. It is her favorite place to escape all the chaos. Except she doesn't look as if it worked."

Samuel swung around. The moment he saw her face Samuel knew she had been inside the barn. "Luke! Adam!"

Callie turned to him. "Samuel? What's wrong? You look as upset as your Ma. What is it?"

"I'll have to explain later, Callie."

Luke and Adam were closing in on the Youngs. When they heard his voice, they both swung around to where Samuel stared.

The three brothers looked at each other.

Nora had heard every single word they said in the barn.

By the look on her face, the secret was out.

The secret was no longer a secret.

Chapter 8

Melody stood on one side of Callie while Abigail stood on her other side, rubbing her belly and staring at the scene in front of them.

"What's wrong with Nora?" Abigail asked. "What's wrong with our men?"

"Oh, dear God in heaven above!" Melody's jaw dropped. "She knows," her voice whispered.

"Knows what? Melody, what in the world is going on here?" Callie knew something was going on. She had noticed earlier in the day. Now it looked as if everything was coming to a head. Whatever it was, she wasn't going to let Samuel go through this alone.

She took a step towards Samuel when Melody's hand shot out. "No, stay here. Please. I'll explain later."

Callie was frustrated. "That's exactly what Samuel just said."

Callie was drawn to Nora's tall frame slowly and meticulously making her way towards her three sons. Her face was unreadable. When she stood in front of them, she gave each one a steady look and then turned to the Youngs.

What was this all about? Callie, growing frustrated, wanted to be by Samuel's side but Melody held on to her hand so she wasn't able to move near her husband.

Most of the other guests were unaware the tension was so high right now. In the background, laughter and little children's voices carried through the air. Callie tried once again to take a step towards her husband but Melody was not letting her go. "Please, wait," she begged Callie.

It was getting harder to comply. When she got a glance of Samuel's face, Callie gasped. He was utterly and totally horrified. Melody grasped harder on her hand. Luke and Adam had the same look.

Nora stood in front of the Youngs. "Widow Young," she said, her voice hard. Callie hadn't ever heard the sound of her voice sounding so harsh. Nora had been so kind the few times she spoke. "I understand you've been accepting monies from my sons for the last ten years or so, ever since my late husband died."

The widow's eyes widened. "I, um, Nora, look, can we talk somewhere private?"

"Not right now." Nora smiled except it didn't appear as a smile at all. Her eyes looked empty. She took a step forward to stare at the widow's teenage sons, first Wesley and then Russell. They stood tall, didn't even blink. Oh, dear Lord, was this what Callie thought it was?

How in the world had this secret been kept silent for so long?

"I do see the resemblance." She wasn't really talking to any one person in particular. For a moment Callie thought she was going to walk away but then she turned to her sons, who looked terribly nervous.

"You were right about me getting too close to them. I can absolutely see Robert in their faces."

"Ma." Luke tried to step forward.

She put up her hand and shook her head.

Luke stopped.

Adam and Samuel stepped forward at the same time then stopped when Luke did.

Instead, Nora turned to Widow Young. "You've been taking money all these years from my sons to keep quiet about your affair. You consorted to blackmail to keep this from me."

Widow Young opened her mouth, closed it and opened it again. "They begged me not to tell you about the boys. I thought I was doing the right thing."

Nora lifted her hand and slapped the Widow across her face. She cried out. Her sons came to her rescue, glaring at Nora. "That was not necessary," Wesley yelled out.

Samuel stepped forward. "Ma, please."

Nora shrugged him off. Callie broke away from Melody and stood by her husband's side. Her hand touched his sleeve. "Samuel," she whispered, letting him know she was right by his side. He gazed at her for a moment then turned back to the scene at hand.

"I've known about the affair since it happened so many years ago." She turned to her sons. "Your father was so guilt ridden he confessed one night and swore he would make it up to me. Then he died. I've been wanting to slap her face for the last ten years for allowing this one night to happen after I was helping to put food on her table. Why did you think we haven't spoken in all that time? It was because I knew! I didn't feel inclined to explain why to my sons! I never planned to tell you my business!"

"What about Wesley and Russell? You didn't know about them!"

"I didn't know about them. No one paid much attention to when they were born, except it was sometime after her husband died. Everyone assumed they belonged to her dead husband. How wrong we all were. How wrong to have forgiven him. He knew. He knew they were his sons. He had to."

"I'm sorry, Ma."

"Ma, I'm so sorry."

"Ma."

She turned to her boys. "You've kept this secret from me all these years. I don't know how I feel. Angry. Hurt. Devastated. Bitter. All I know is I have to get away from every single one of you."

She turned to the widow. "Don't you ever step foot on my land again. You fornicated with my husband and then accepted money as a bribe to keep your dirty deeds silent. Widow Young, shame on you! You've gotten all the money from my sons you will ever receive. If your boys need something, have them come see me. All of you had better steer clear of me for awhile. I don't want to speak to anyone right now!"

Callie watched as Nora stomped her way across the yard towards the house. She held herself tall, nodding to others as she passed by as if there was no exchange of words that just happened. Rusty touched her arm, speaking quietly to her while Nora nodded and then went inside.

Callie wanted to run after her, tell Nora something to make her feel better but her place was here with her husband. She turned to Samuel. "It will all work out. She's upset and angry right now. Give her time."

He gathered Callie close. "We tried to protect her from this and now look, it happened anyway." He hung his head in shame.

Callie saw the devastated looks on each brothers face.

<> <>

Samuel thought his Ma would at least be at the breakfast table in the morning but she was not leaving her room. Callie, Abigail and Melody had taken over, making breakfast for everyone. The hands came in as was their routine, standing behind their chair to bow their heads before sitting down to pass around the plates of eggs and flapjacks.

His head hurt this morning. Considering he hadn't slept much at all last night, he needed to apologize for leaving Callie alone. He'd wait until the meal was over. "Would you like to join me for a walk to the orchard this morning, Callie?"

She looked right at him, her broad smile lighting up his mood. If anything, Callie's sweet presence may help. "Of course. If you don't mind waiting on the porch, I'll help to clean up first."

A half hour later, she came outside while he paced back and forth. His two brothers had already went out to the southern end, checking the fences while Samuel stayed behind. He had promised he'd catch up later. He needed to speak with Callie before doing anything else. Or, making any more mistakes.

He took her hand as they walked towards the orchard. She pointed upward. "The apples look as if they are ready to fall."

"I can pick some for you if you'd like to make some pies?"

Callie laughed. "I think you are hinting at something, sir. Would you like some apple pie for dessert?"

Samuel pulled her close, placing an arm around her slim waist. "I think that is an excellent choice."

She turned to him. "I don't recall having much of a say in the matter. I believe you and the apples are in cahoots."

He looked up and winked at the apples hanging from the branches. He reached out and pulled one off, then held it to his ear. "Yes, uh huh. I believe so. You want to be a pie?"

Callie giggled. She placed a kiss on his mouth. "Samuel White, you are a little devil. Of course I'll make an apple pie just for you!"

He coughed. "Well, there's the thing. If you make just one apple pie, the whole ranch will be fighting for a slice of it and I may not get even one piece!"

She stepped back and glared at him, even though her voice was full of mirth. "Samuel! I've been on a working ranch before! Did you honestly think I'd make only one pie? Well, how am I going to keep up my reputation as a wonderful, delightful wife of one of the owners if I only made one pie?"

"You are too far away from me," he told her as he pulled her close. His kiss deepened before he released her. "Sounds like I am keeping you away, Mrs. White. Maybe I should let you get back to making those pies."

She went back into his arms and gave him a long, drawn out kiss that lasted for quite some time. His arms tightened. He could do this all day. He knew she wanted to talk about last night and to be honest, he didn't want to right now. All he wanted was to hold her close. But, Callie was his wife now and he would include her no matter what.

"Samuel. Before you say a word, I know how devastated you were last night. Starting our marriage on the sour note of last evening was not what I wanted. I know you were distracted. Let's get through this and start over."

Samuel covered her cheek with feathered kisses. "I do love you, Callie. You're smart, beautiful and considerate. I know I picked the right bride even if you were originally meant for Adam."

She laughed. "I wasn't meant for Adam. We are two of a kind, Mr. White. While you are working out things with your family, I'll offer you my shoulder to lean on. And pie."

Samuel picked her up off the ground and swung her around. She giggled, shaking a fist at him. "Let me down, sir! I have pie to bake!"

They spent the next hour picking apples between sweet kisses and hugs. If anyone was able to see them, well, Samuel figured they'd know how much in love they were. It was pretty obvious to anyone who bothered to pay attention.

After filling her apron with a load of apples, Samuel walked Callie back to the house. He gave her one last kiss before heading out to meet his brothers.

He gazed towards his Ma's room, where the door was firmly closed. For a moment, he was tempted to try to go see her but at the last moment he turned away, gave his wife one more kiss and left, tipping his hat to Abigail and Melody who were working on the next meal. Time would tell if his Ma would ever forgive them.

<><>

Callie began to work alongside her sister-in-laws, dropping the apples into a basket. "What will we do about Nora?"

Abigail looked worried. "I tried several times to lure Nora out. She hasn't eaten anything at all today. I'm sick with concern for her."

"It's an awful thing to find out after all these years," Melody admitted. "I knew."

Callie and Abigail turned to her. "What do you mean you knew? About the secret?"

Melody nodded. "I'm not proud of that fact. Years ago when I would visit each summer with my parents, I overheard the brothers talking. They didn't know I was in the barn. It was one of the reasons I married Tommy's father."

Abigail frowned. "I never knew this. What happened?"

Melody kept her voice down. Even though Nora was hiding in her room, the walls were not real thick. "The brothers made a pact they would never marry. They were afraid if they did, more people would know about the secret and it would become too difficult to keep it from Nora. When I overheard them, I was madly in love with Adam. But knowing what I did, when Thomas became interested, I didn't think I ever had a chance with Adam."

Callie finished for her. "So you married Thomas and later found out Adam was willing to marry after all?"

Melody gave her a lop-sided grin. "Something like that. It was a bit more complicated. But, I have him now and can't wait to start a family."

Abigail rubbed her belly. She hadn't said much before now. "I know Luke is heartbroken. It was a hard decision for him to marry, he went through a lot of emotions and turmoil because he didn't want to marry. Now, after all he's been through, Nora won't talk to anyone. Rusty said she told him to leave her be, that she needs some time alone."

Callie nodded. "I do believe that is exactly what we need to do. Let her grieve. It is a terrible situation. All we can do is love our husbands and stand by them. This will blow over soon."

Abigail agreed. "I hate to see her so devastated though."

Melody argued they should try to coerce her out of the room.

"For now, let's leave her be. I'm new here and don't want her to resent me by trying to force her into something she doesn't want right now. I think I can grow to love Nora White." Callie meant every single word. She was anxious to have a relationship with her mother-in-law and hoped everyone came to their senses soon.

"Ladies, we will have to take over until Nora decides to come out of hiding. We better have a plan of action." Melody was right. They needed to work together.

Callie set a bowl of apples on the table. "I can start breakfast since I'm already in the house."

Melody nodded. "I'll be up to help you and then I can start preparing lunch. Since most of the hands are out in the field, we will make sandwiches or something light for the ones here. Rusty and the rest of the men won't mind."

Abigail sat down beside them at the table. "I'm willing to do whatever you need done. I'm not sure I can do as much as the both of you put together. My physical body is winded by the end of the afternoon."

Callie saw the problem. "Melody and I can handle breakfast and lunch. Why don't you peel potatoes for the supper meal. You can sit at the table or on the porch and won't have to do any cooking. I'll take over that job."

Are you sure, Callie? You just got married. I'm sure you want to spend time with your new husband."

She shook her head. "There will be plenty of time to do so, but for right now we all have to pull together and make this work. Sooner or later Nora will come out of her room and we don't want to have a mess for her to clean up. Let's show her how well we work together."

The three women clasped hands. "Sisters helping sisters."

She wasn't sure if it was Abigail or Melody who said that but her hand was right there in the midst of it all. She had sisters at last. It was a great feeling.

Chapter 9

She slid out of bed, leaving Samuel to sleep. Her movements usually woke him up anyway and then he'd pull her back under the covers until she'd give him morning kisses.

Not today. He never even heard her get up. After quickly dressing, she made her way downstairs to the kitchen. She had waited up for Samuel last night and it had been late until they fell asleep. Figuring she'd have to hurry if breakfast was going to be on time, she hurried over to Nora's door.

Callie picked up the full tray, frowning. It had been five days since Nora had retreated to her room without a word to anyone. Every single night, she left a tray for her mother-in-law only to find it untouched the next morning. At lunch, Abigail would knock and knock but Nora refused to answer. All three of her boys tried to talk her into coming out but they failed. She'd mutter for them to let her be.

Melody came in just as Callie fired up the cook stove. "Still no luck with Nora. Her tray hasn't been touched."

The two set about getting breakfast ready with heavy hearts. They tried over and over again to lure Nora out but nothing seemed to work. Callie worried Nora was ill. "Should we barge in to check on her? I'm getting worried, Melody. She can't go on like this."

"I'll talk to Adam. He was outside her door last night while you and Samuel took a walk. Nora spoke a few words so she must be fine."

"I'm still terribly worried. Maybe she comes out to get something to eat after everyone is in bed. I don't know, but why wouldn't she take what's on the tray?"

Melody giggled. "Maybe she doesn't like our cooking."

Her words brought a smile to Callie's face. "Thank you. I'm taking this so serious, aren't I?"

"We all are. Besides, it is serious but we have to give her time. She has learned her husband wasn't the loyal person she thought he was. I remember Mr. White. He was a nice, hard working man. He loved his wife and his boys. I find it hard to believe what happened so can you imagine how she feels?"

Callie nodded in understanding. "You do have a good point. I guess we have to be patient."

Samuel stood at the top of the stairs stretching, then made his way downstairs. "I smell something delicious."

Callie looked up at him. She thought *he* looked quite delicious but didn't say it out loud. Her cheeks pinkened at the thought. She was being too bold in her thoughts of him. "Breakfast will be ready in five minutes. Take a chair, Samuel."

He sauntered over to Callie who was flipping the cakes over the hot stove. Wrapping his arms around her waist, he placed a kiss on her neck. "Good morning, Callie."

His kisses were feather light against her neck but it made her tingle from the touch. "Behave yourself, husband. I have work to do."

Samuel's low growl was meant for her ears only but Melody made a tsk, tsk sound before he left her to stand by his regular chair. The others poured in ready to eat.

"Looks like everyone is here," Callie called out. Their heads bowed like they did every morning while the prayer was said aloud by Adam. Plates began to shift back and forth as chairs scooted around and flapjacks were passed around the table.

Ranch hands quickly ate then filed out one by one to start their day. Callie was getting ready to start the clean up when Samuel made an announcement. "I spoke with Melody and Abigail. They are going to relieve you of your duties this morning."

Callie shook her head. "I can't let them finish the work alone. Abigail is expecting."

Samuel raised an eyebrow. "You didn't even ask why."

She set the dishes in soapy water. "Okay, why?"

"I have a surprise in store for you. Are you ready?"

"Samuel, did you not hear what I said! I can't go and leave this work to my sisters to finish. It's too much."

"Okay then, I'll be back for you in one hour. Will that suffice?"

Abigail and Melody pushed Samuel out the door. "Go on Samuel. Come back in an hour. Callie will be ready."

"What are you two ladies up to?"

"Samuel informed us he wants to take you for a ride and show you the ranch. There are some very romantic spots on the White Ranch and you are not going to miss out."

"Well then, I guess we best stop talking and start working because I'm not going to leave and have you ladies finish all the work."

An hour later, Callie flung the dirty apron in the wash bin and freshened up. She pushed her hair back except for the blonde tendrils that always escaped. Pinching her cheeks, she looked in the small mirror over the night stand, satisfied she looked approachable.

Callie went outside to wait for Samuel. Melody ran out and handed her a basket. "A little something for lunch. Enjoy," she told her before going back inside so Callie wasn't able to refuse.

Samuel led two horses right up to the porch. "Your ride awaits," he told her.

She was excited to ride the range with Samuel even though she should stay at the house and help the others. It took the three of them to keep the kitchen going. How had Nora done it alone all these years?

Now that she had time to think about things, she hadn't had much time with Samuel at all. Except for their evening walk last night, these past few days were spent worrying about his Ma and taking over the kitchen. She was sure Samuel needed this break as much as she did.

It would be good for them to get out on the range and forget about their worries.

Callie looked over to see Samuel giving her one of those devil may care looks. His grin told her one thing. He wanted to have some fun. Well, she was going to give him what he wanted.

She pointed. "Race you across the field, all the way to those oaks down yonder!"

"Winner gets prize of choice," he teased.

"Then I'll be sure to win!" She hollered once before her heels dug in as the mare took off without a backward glance. Callie raced side by side with Samuel. Her hair loosened and she lifted her face into the wind. Before she knew what was going on they were down by the oak trees. She had gotten there first but had a feeling he let her win.

"Let's walk the horses for awhile."

"I won. Aren't you going to say so," she teased him back.

"It's because I let you win."

"I highly doubt that, Mr. White."

He moved his horse closer so there was a hair's space between them right before he pulled her from the saddle and plopped her down in front of him. Samuel twisted his head and kissed her deeply. Her arms went around his neck. "Now that's what I call a prize," she told him, her smiles lighting up her face.

They walked the horses for some time until they came to a field where the grass grew along the creek bank. Running water ran across stones and rocky areas. It was the perfect place for a picnic. Samuel took a rolled up blanket from his saddle and laid it out on the creek bank while Callie placed the basket she was given on the blanket before taking a seat.

Samuel sat across from her. "What's in the basket? I'm famished."

"Let's see what Melody and Abigail sent along." Fried chicken, rolls and a slice of yesterday's apple pie made for a great lunch. As they enjoyed their meal, Callie wondered why he wasn't out on the range with his brothers. Perhaps they all needed some time to digest everything that happened. "Where is Luke and Adam?"

Samuel shrugged. "Guess they are working. I was ordered to take the day off, spend it with you since we did the same thing for my brothers when they were first married. Let's enjoy today since tomorrow I'll be back on the range, away from you."

Callie didn't want to bring the subject up but knew they had to discuss Nora. "What will we do about your Ma, Samuel? We can't let her stay in her room forever."

Samuel gave her a worried look. "Ma is going to come out of there and be a stronger woman than ever. You wait and see. She's been brought to her knees but she'll bounce back, I promise. Now let's forget about her and concentrate on you and me."

He was right. She leaned over to place a kiss on his mouth. He grabbed her and pulled her onto his lap. "Samuel!"

His kisses began to get more serious. She looked around. "What if someone rides up here and sees us like this?" Callie was adventurous but this was perhaps too bold of a move.

He nuzzled her neck. "No one will. We have the whole day to ourselves, you and me, alone, here on this creek bank. I can guarantee none of my brothers or any ranch hands will ride up this way today. Forget the world, Callie, it's you and me, right here, right now."

Well, since he put it like that, she began to kiss him like he won the grand prize.

<> <>

Callie wasn't able to stop laughing. Or smiling. Or giggling. This was a wonderful afternoon and Samuel had spent the day making her realize how lucky she was. She turned to him. "Thank you, Samuel. I almost hate to go back."

"I do, too. But reality is just around the corner. Or a picnic, look at the yard." Two large tables were covered with dishes. "It looks as if Rusty is roasting some meat outside. I bet he got himself a deer this afternoon."

"I didn't know he hunted?"

"He's probably upset about Ma and doesn't know what to do, like all of us. At times he'll head out alone but then he always shoots us a good meal."

Callie turned to him. "This is upsetting everyone here."

Samuel agreed. "We are all worried about her. Every single person here. I listened to the hands this morning. Cody, Roger and Matt wanted to break down the door and force her to come out of the bedroom to talk about things. Rusty, the old codger, he gave them all a talking to and said if anyone broke down her door he'd fire them."

"Does he have the authority to fire someone?"

Samuel shrugged. "Rusty is the oldest member of our thrown-together family. So, I'd say yes."

"It looks like the men are all cleaning up to get ready for supper. Perhaps I should go see if I can help bring the food out." She slid from the saddle, not waiting for Samuel to help. It was much easier to get around wearing blue jeans but had retired them since she was getting so much attention when she wore her pretty dresses. Today she was glad she wore a dress. It made her smile thinking of their afternoon together.

Samuel took the reins from her hands, leaned over and gave her a long, drawn out kiss. Before he walked away he looked deep in her eyes. "I love you," he whispered.

She began to walk backwards, watching as he led the horses into the barn. All of a sudden, he turned. She giggled and then blew him a kiss. Lifting his hand, he pretended to catch it and placed his hand across his own heart. Callie about melted. He was the one who would always melt her heart.

It was time to get serious. Abigail was working hard even though it was difficult for her. Callie jumped in and scooped up the bowls to take outside. It looked as if they were having a feast. "What's the occasion?"

Melody grinned. "While you were out gallivanting with your lover, you missed all the action. Nora asked for Rusty when he got back this afternoon. He came out of her room, announced they were having a picnic out in the yard. He said Nora would join us."

Callie's heart jumped at the news. The boys would be so happy. Everyone would be happy. It was going to be a great day now that Nora had a change of heart. She was certain they would all do whatever it takes to help Nora get through this. Besides, she was anxious to work side by side with the woman who was going to become like a mother to her.

Her excitement grew as Samuel finally came out of the barn. He would be happy to hear the news. She almost ran across the yard to tell him until his brothers fell in beside Samuel. One of them jumped up and took down the other brother, while the last one jumped on the two who were down and a wrestling match began again.

Abigail stopped what she was doing to watch. "I swear they act like they are ten years old!" She said it with a smile though.

Melody stared before she set down a large bowl. "No telling when those boys will grow up. Abigail, your poor child will grow up to watch these men and their shenanigans."

"That's not so bad. It could be a lot worse," Abigail said. "I think it's rather adorable."

Melody giggled. "Me too. Sometimes I want to jump in and wrestle, too!"

Callie grinned. "That's scandalous, Melody!"

Melody chirped, "Says the one who wears those fancy, revealing blue jeans!"

"I'll let you borrow them sometime. You will be amazed how they feel and how easy it is to get work done."

"That's a deal. I better get the rolls and we'll be ready to sit down."

Callie nodded. "I'll ring the bell. Abigail please sit down, you look exhausted."

Abigail did as she was told. When her husband looked up from the ground he jumped up and began to walk towards her. He was so devoted to his sweet wife. Callie knew Samuel would be the same way if and when she became pregnant.

She gave the rope a tug and caught everyone's attention with the first sound. "Supper is served," she called out even though she didn't have to. Most of the hands were already standing behind the chairs, waiting to dig in.

Samuel took Callie's hand and kissed it before escorting her to the table. There was a seat at the head of the table. Everyone stood silent as they waited for Nora.

It was a matter of moments before she pushed the screen door open and appeared on the porch. Instead of her usual cotton dress, she appeared in a riding habit with a matching jacket, a high-collared chemisette and skirt. She made her way to the table and stood by her chair without speaking to anyone.

Callie noticed her husband's knuckles whiten as he clutched the back of the chair. She chanced looking at his brothers to see the same thing, all three had been hanging on to their chairs in anticipation of Nora's entrance. Callie wanted to let it play out but she also wanted Samuel to know she was right here for him, always.

Her hand went to his arm. It was stiff and rigid but the moment she touched him, he sighed. She leaned in to whisper in his ear. "It will be alright."

Looking up, Callie noticed Abigail and Melody did the same thing with their husbands. It was as if the three of them were on the same page, they all knew something was about to happen and had to let their husbands know they were standing with them, no matter what.

Why was Nora dressed as if she were leaving? It scared Callie and yet she realized maybe the woman needed to get away. It was her choice. She was a grown woman. Callie wondered how the ranch would get by if Nora wasn't here to keep everyone in line.

"I'll start the prayer," she announced in her no-nonsense tone. *"Lord, thank you for each and every one of the people standing at this table today. We all have our own journey to go down and knowing you are behind us and with us lessens the load. Thank you, Lord, for each and every day there is breath in our bodies. Thank you for this food, for friends and family and most of all, Lord, thank you for giving us this life we live. Amen."*

Callie and Samuel glanced at each other. Yes, there was something going on. He did the same with his brothers before they all sat down to eat.

As usual, plates were passed around the table but not quite as livid as before. It was almost as if everyone knew there was something in the air. Rusty was the only one who behaved like his normal self, cracking jokes and handing out sarcastic comments.

After the food was all but gone, Nora wrapped a fork against her glass. "I have an announcement to make."

Both tables were so silent the only thing heard was an occasional noise from the barn. Callie swore even the birds stopped chirping.

"Ma, is everything alright?" Samuel asked.

Luke leaned back in his chair. "I second that," he told her.

Adam nodded. "Ma, what's going on?"

She smiled at each one. "You boys are way too serious. First of all, I'd like to thank each and every one of you for all of the concern. I wasn't able to get a moments rest in my bedroom as everyone kept banging on the door, wondering if I am okay."

She stood up at the head of the table and lifted her glass. "I want to propose a toast to all of you. Thank you for all of your concerns." The others lifted their glasses and drank, a few mutters heard here and there.

Samuel squeezed Callie's hand. She gazed at him. "I love you," she whispered in his ear. His thumb began to trace an imaginary line back and forth on her hand. He was so nervous for Ma's announcement, but she was there to hold him up, no matter what Nora would say.

"Ma, you are stalling," her oldest muttered. It was clear Luke was angry and upset at the same time. He was the most dramatic of the brothers.

"I am. So let me get down to business. I am leaving the ranch."

Luke stood up.

Adam stood next.

Samuel followed.

"Leaving, but what about my baby? Our baby! Oh, no, Nora! I can't have a baby without you!" Abigail became distraught. Luke took her in his arms and held her, speaking softly in her ear.

"Ma, you are talking nonsense. What do you mean you are leaving here?" It was Adams turn to be annoyed. He held Melody's hand in his, gritting his teeth while pulling her closer.

"Boys, don't get so excited. I'm taking a holiday, if you want to call it something. A sabbatical for what it's worth. I've been on this ranch for the last thirty plus years, dedicated to see it succeed. I want some time to digest all that has happened in the last week. We have done well. All of you boys have a wife now to stand by your side and I am pleased with each and every one of you."

Callie let a tear fall.

Abigail and Melody did the same.

She addressed the ranch hands. "Cody, Roger, Matt, you have all helped this ranch to grow. I am gifting you with a bonus and hope you continue to be the best ranch hands this side of the Texas border. Rusty, my old friend, I will miss your daily accounts of life here but I will be back. I promise."

She stepped away from the head of the table to stand in front of Luke her first born. "You have a special place in my heart as my first son and will make your place at the head of the table now. I expect you to make sure this ranch doesn't fall apart without me." She held him close then turned to his wife. "Abigail, I won't be gone forever and will meet my grand child soon. I promise. Thank you for making my son happy."

Adam turned to his Ma, giving her a hug. "I'll miss you Ma even though I know you have to do this. Where will you go?"

"I don't know yet. I'm going to take it one day at a time. There is so much to see and do. I want some freedom, away from here and I hope you understand. You've always been my favorite, you know."

Luke held his mother tight, laughing at her remark about being the favorite, something she told all three of them. Callie watched, her eyes filling with unshed tears.

Melody held onto Nora for the longest time. "You've been a daughter to me, perhaps a bit more than the others. I'm glad you came back here, where you will always have a home. You and Tommy are always a big part of my life."

Nora picked up Tommy and gave him a hug. He hugged her back and slid from her arms so fast she laughed out loud. He was so busy playing with the wooden toy one of his uncles bought him, he really didn't know what was going on. Callie was sure Nora was glad she didn't have to explain anything to the child.

It was time for Samuel to say goodbye to his Ma. He gathered her in his arms and held onto her.

"You are my youngest, my baby. Your laughter has kept me sane for all those times I wanted to give up. Thank you, Samuel for your spark and adventurous spirit. You've found the perfect match with Callie. I love you all so much."

Callie let the tears fall. She ran into Nora's open arms and said her goodbyes. She didn't know how long Nora would be gone or when she'd return but she did know one thing. Callie would always be here, waiting for the day she returned.

Samuel let go of his Ma as she turned away from them all. "I love you all, this ranch and my home. I will be back." With those words, she took her place on the wagon Rusty had loaded for her earlier in the day. Waving, she made her way down the road on her next journey.

Callie stood alongside her husband. The crowd at the table was so quiet as Nora left it was almost as if someone had died. She had to fix this. After all, Nora left the women here to take over while she was gone.

"Don't look so glum, everyone. Nora is happy, let's be happy for her. It's something she wants to do." There were some nods and then everyone began to chat amongst each other. " Who wants cake?"

Shouts erupted at the mention of cake.

Abigail's eyes widened. "We don't have cake," she mouthed.

"Oh, yes we do!" Melody waved them inside. "Come on, ladies. Let's get these men some cake. We need to celebrate."

Callie followed the two inside, curious.

"We have cake because I've been so upset all day I baked two big cakes!"

They cut up slices and passed them out to everyone. It seemed as if everyone's lives would get back to normal. Nora may be gone but she'd be back. Her promise had reassured everyone there.

Callie walked up to her husband, where he stood to the side of the crowd, staring at the two cabins across the way.

"I was going to tell you we'd start on our own cabin soon."

She turned to him. "Oh, Samuel. We can start building right away. Nora won't be gone forever. Then we will have our own place by the time she returns."

"I feel lost, Callie. My heart is cold. It's empty and it's our fault she found out. We tried so hard to keep from hurting her. Ma was all we had these past years and now we've gone and ruined everything for her."

Callie shook her head. "No, you haven't. Look at her." She pointed to the wagon as it made its way down the long, narrow road. "She's going on an adventure, one she well deserves. It's high time Nora did something for herself. Besides, she's not alone. It looks like Matt is along for the ride. Rusty told us it was the agreement they made. A woman can't travel alone."

Samuel stared at the wagon until it disappeared from view. Then he smiled at Callie. "I bet between finding a place to go for her adventure and feeding Matt, she'll be back sooner than later. That man loves to eat."

She laughed out loud, realizing Samuel was accepting things at last. They had a new path to take, one filled with love, adventure and family.

He picked her up and swung her around. "I love you, Callie White."

She placed a kiss on his mouth. "I love you, Samuel White. I'm ready for another adventure. What say you?"

He threw back his head and laughed. "I'm ready for any adventure if it has to do with you, my lovely wife."

He whispered in her ear.

She gasped.

Then she slid from his arms and ran towards the barn. "The winner gets to pick the prize."

"Then maybe I'll let you win."

"I always win," she fired back.

Their laughter rang out over the White land as they closed the barn doors behind them.

<> <>

Thanks for reading Samuel and Callie's story. I was going to stop after the last son found a wife but my readers insisted on Nora's story and I like to keep my readers happy.....

Nora is at a loss what to do next. Confused and hurt at the most recent news, she needs some time away from the ranch and everyone she holds dear. Where will she go and how will this affect the one person who has always been in love with Nora?

Get A Groom for Nora - Available NOW![1]

(https://www.amazon.com/Groom-Nora-Book-Sons-White-ebook/

dp/B07BXTCH2T/

ref=as_li_ss_tl?ie=UTF8&qid=1522925511&sr=8-

2&keywords=a+groom+for+nora&linkCode=ll1&tag=keysvaca-

20&linkId=3939311f64cbfbd4e1f7c4ed5f0ec1af)

1. https://www.amazon.com/Groom-Nora-Book-Sons-White-

ebook/dp/B07BXTCH2T/

ref=as_li_ss_tl?ie=UTF8&qid=1522925511&sr=8-

2&keywords=a+groom+for+nora&linkCode=ll1&tag=keysva

ca-20&linkId=3939311f64cbfbd4e1f7c4ed5f0ec1af

Want a free book?

Go to Cyndiraye.com[2]

Click on the above website to be notified when a new book comes out or enter for some great fun and prizes, don't forget to sign up!

Keep reading for a free chapter of An Outlaw's Honor, the first book in the Brides of Mill Ridge series...

Free Chapter An Outlaw's Honor

Have you read the fascinating stories about the folks from Mill Ridge? A spin-off from the original Bride of Wichita Falls series, Mill Ridge was an outlaw town at one time. With the help of townsfolk from Wichita Falls, the sheriff cleaned up the town and began to turn it into a place where interesting characters and family would be happy to build a new life. Here's a chapter from An Outlaw's Honor, the first in the Mill Ridge series:

An Outlaw's Honor
"Look out for your own"
-the code of the west

"Good morning, Miss Addie! What brings you to Mill Ridge so early?" Elizabeth was happy to see her mentor at the front door even if the older woman seemed to be in a state of agitation. Her dark well-kept hair was askew, along with a few strands out of place. Elizabeth noted her being a bit out of sorts for the well-managed woman everyone knew and loved.

Miss Addie took off her riding gloves as she stepped in to the foyer of the boarding house. She looked around. "You've done an excellent job here, Elizabeth. I know taking over for Sophie so quickly was difficult and I promise to send you off as a mail order bride soon, you have my word."

Elizabeth welcomed the woman with a hug. "Please, sit and have some tea."

The pot was steaming on the stove. Elizabeth was always up before her guests, planning out the days meals and making sure everything was in order for breakfast. As soon as Rose, her helper and partner for the time being, finished her early morning work, the two would start breakfast.

She poured two cups of tea, setting them on the table, along with a porcelain bowl filled with sugar and a fresh cup of cream. After serving, she sat down to wait for Miss Addie to begin. She knew it was fruitless to ask the older woman any questions until they had their tea. Her curiosity was piqued.

"How is Sophie adjusting to married life with our new sheriff, Salem Nightingale?" Miss Addie didn't seem to be in a hurry now that she was settled in at the table.

Elizabeth took a sip of tea. She had replaced Sophie, who managed the boarding house up until she married a law man. "Wonderful, she spent the first few weeks after her honeymoon teaching me the ropes about match-making and running this place. So far I've matched a farmer with one of our wonderful ladies. Jocelyn is so happy with Fred Williams. Then there is Nanette, she's the quiet one in the crowd, she married Jonathan Myers, one of the workers at the mill. I'm very happy you are allowing me to be a matchmaker, Miss Addie, although I'll never be quite as good as you when it comes to this position."

Miss Addie shook her head. "Oh don't be prudent. You do a fine job, everyone tells me so. I'm sure you will have every chance to match up every single man in this town and beyond."

Elizabeth smiled. "If I did that, I would be out of a job."

"Nonsense, you will be married off by then to a wonderful man. When you took this position to help get the boarding house and matchmaking service started here in Mill Ridge, I promised to fulfil your original request to find you a wonderful husband, and I will."

"You are right. Miss Addie. Thank you for the kind words. I believe our Rose is sweet on one of our boarders. And, Reverend Pope feels the same way about her. She is next in line for a husband, but it may turn out I won't have to do any matchmaking after all. If you would like, please send over two more ladies for me to work with. I will begin my work with them immediately. Perhaps we will wait to see what happens between Rose and the Reverend."

"I'm impressed, Elizabeth. When we rescued all of the women from that horrible man awhile back, I had no idea so many would still be here. I was certain all of the girls would go back to their prospective homes. I'm happy to say nine of you stayed. Which is a wonderful thing since there are so many single men that need a good wife. We will build this town up just like we did Wichita Falls."

"There isn't too many women here and it can be lonely for some of us. If it weren't for Rose and Sophie, and the two ladies we just matched up, this town would be all men. We have to fix it soon, Miss Addie. Can you send me two more mail order brides? I have two extra rooms at the moment. I can place two ladies in one room and rent the other spare room out."

"Of course, if you feel ready to take on more, I'll send them over tomorrow. I think I know which two are ready to become brides. My boarding house is filled up and the five ladies left have to share rooms, making it difficult to keep tempers in check at times. Now, the reason I am truly here is to see Sheriff Nightingale. It seems a man rode in to our town last night asking to be directed to Mill Ridge. I was hoping I beat him here since he wasn't up and about when I left this morning."

"I've been up since daylight and haven't seen or heard anyone trek through," Elizabeth answered. "Why the concern?"

"He had the looks of an outlaw. I don't want to alarm anyone but I got the impression he was on a serious quest. He was looking for someone specific. He was asking questions and showing a photo of a woman."

Elizabeth smiled. "No worries then, there are only a few women here. Sophie is happily married, tucked away in the Sheriff's cottage and Rose and I are the only two other women in town. Jocelyn and Nanette live outside of town. I wonder who he is looking for?"

"Perhaps he is here to stir up trouble and yet I don't get that awful feeling about him I usually do when someone bad passes through."

"Well, you go on and see the Sheriff. I'll need to get breakfast started. It's been a pleasure to have you here."

The moment she spoke the words, Rose came tumbling down the steps. The girl was so clumsy, she almost fell down the last three. She came in to the kitchen like a whirlwind, all smiles and tucking strands of hair in her bun. Elizabeth had sent her up to tidy the empty rooms earlier in case a guest arrived without notice, which almost always happened.

"Miss Addie! So nice to see you." Rose gave her mentor a hug, while Elizabeth looked on in amusement. The girl was simply a mess.

"Good day, ladies," Miss Addie told them before rushing out to find the sheriff.

Elizabeth turned to Rose. "Really, young lady, can you please go and straighten your hair. It looks as if you haven't combed it."

Rose giggled. "I haven't. I woke up late and pushed it back out of the way. Reverend Pope seems to think I am adorable."

"He told you that?" Elizabeth was shocked. When had the reverend been talking like that to Rose? She would need to keep a better eye on the two. After all, Elizabeth took it upon herself to mentor Rose and get her ready for her stint as a mail-order bride. If Reverend Pope wanted to marry her, he'd have to say so before Elizabeth put any time or effort into finding Rose a husband.

Rose giggled again, placing a pan on the stove. She began to crack the eggs in to the pan, one by one. "He always tells me how beautiful I am, and that I have an inspiring smile."

"He shouldn't be telling you those things in private, Rose. He needs to say if he wants to court you."

Rose sighed. "Oh, how wonderful that would be. I am afraid I'm falling for the good reverend."

"The reverend is here in the boarding house until his sanctuary is ready. The church is being re-built and the sanctuary will be done shortly. No flirting with the good man, Rose. In the meantime, Miss Addie said there is a stranger coming to town. He was in Wichita Falls last night and is looking for a woman. Steer clear of any strangers, Rose."

"I will, Elizabeth." The younger Rose turned to Elizabeth. "Please don't worry. The reverend hasn't done anything damaging. He's a man of God and his kind words were always spoken on the porch in public."

"I'm relieved to hear this, Rose. I'm afraid we may be short on eggs this morning. I see the good doctor is in town so I'm going to go over to see if I can buy some from his stock he keeps in the back yard. I shall only be about twenty minutes at the most."

"Take the empty basket and fill it up, please. We may need a few more this morning as I plan to bake a cake this afternoon."

Elizabeth took the basket, swinging the handle as she left the boarding house. Rose was going to bake a cake for the reverend after he had mentioned his love of chocolate cake. She smiled to herself. Oh, how wonderful it would be to have the growing excitement of a new love.

She didn't think she'd ever fall in love again. Perhaps Elizabeth was cursed. She had been engaged to a wonderful man. They had grown up together in the same town. Their families spent time together, they all went everywhere together.

When the outlaw gang came to their small town in Kansas, they began to torment the residents. They would rob townsfolk right off the street and no one was able to stand up to them. At first it was mild but when the gang robbed the bank and killed everyone inside, Elizabeth's whole world had changed.

Her mother, father and two younger brothers had been in the bank that day. Her fiancé brother, who owned the bank, was killed, along with his parents and grandmother.

Her fiancé had been out of town, looking over a plot of land he planned to buy. He had saved for two years to buy the land and he had promised her it would be theirs. When he had returned to find his brother and parents dead, along with the others, he had changed overnight.

His behavior had changed as he began sending telegrams to places far away. He spent less time with Elizabeth even though she needed him more than ever. Her whole family was wiped out. She had no one and yet he began to pull away from her no matter what she said or did.

His whole world revolved around waiting for each telegram, then leaving town on his horse for days at a time. His clothing began to get sloppy as if he didn't care what he looked like. Hair that was short and clipped, was now long and choppy, hiding under a wide-brimmed cowboy hat.

Elizabeth became more worried day after day. She watched his looks turn in to one like the outlaws he swore he hated.

Then one day he simply rode out of town. She had watched from her family home as he mounted his horse, knowing deep in her heart it would be the last time she'd ever see him.

The hurt that day was too immense to relive. When she had realized what he was going to do, she ran out the front door, lifting her skirts and striking up dust as she ran as fast as she could to stop him from leaving. "Wait! What are you doing?" She had cried out but he didn't look her in the eye.

"I'm a lost soul, Elizabeth. It's better this way. Go on with your life."

She stood there, willing him to look at her but he kept the brim of his hat low over his eyes. "I love you," she told him. "Doesn't that account for anything?"

A strange man she didn't recognize strolled from the saloon, dusting his hat and placing it on his head. He got on his horse and rode over to the two of them. "Ready?"

Her fiancé nodded. He directed his next words to her. "Love someone else. I'm done with this town and everyone in it."

She charged at him, reaching up to grab his leg. She tried to look up at him but he kept avoiding her eyes. "Why, my love, why? We can get through this together."

"Forget about me, Elizabeth Sheldon. I'm not your kind of man. I don't love you any more."

Shock filled her from the top of her head down to the tips of her boots. Her skirts went flying as she ran back to the haven of her family home, unable to watch the man she loved leave town. *I don't love you any more!* She'd never, ever forget those words as long as she lived.

Elizabeth stumbled as she crossed the street, realizing she was revisiting a part of her past she had shoved under the porch mat over a year ago. Was this job as match-maker causing her to relive her past? Perhaps she should tell Miss Addie to hurry and find her a husband. She closed her eyes for a moment, unsure how to move on. If she married someone else, was it fair to them knowing she'd never be able to love anyone else ever again? Her first attempt at love went horribly wrong, then the mail order bride fiasco fell through when that awful man tried to sell them as slaves. Perhaps it wasn't in the cards for her to be happy.

Realizing it was probably better this way, she decided to tell Miss Addie not to find her a husband. She would stay here, make this home. There was no reason she couldn't run the boarding house and live her life the same as Miss Addie.

"Good morning, Elizabeth. Are you here for some eggs?"

Elizabeth hadn't realized she was standing on the porch of the doctor's office. A few folks were staring. "Good morning, Nurse Ellie. May I buy some please? We're running short."

"Help yourself, Elizabeth. It's busy here today, so just put your money on the counter as you leave. I'm afraid I don't have time to have tea with you."

The good doctor and Nurse Ellie spent two days a week in Mill Ridge to help out until a doctor became available. Miss Addie donated the house and office for the doctor's use since she owned four or five different establishments in Mill Ridge, too. The doctor and his nurse-wife were trying to see all of the patients possible in the two days they had available.

So, Elizabeth was glad Nurse Ellie was too busy to talk. She didn't feel like holding a conversation with anyone today. Bringing up the past even in her mind was too distressing. She fumbled at the door to the back yard, stepping in chicken poop one too many times. After a struggle, Elizabeth collected the eggs she needed, placed the money on the counter and quickly left the doctors office without speaking to any of the patrons waiting on the porch.

"Good day, Elizabeth," Nurse Ellie told her as she came out to gather the next patient.

Elizabeth turned to wave to Nurse Ellie who was staring down the street, a look of awe all over her face. It wasn't normal for the nurse to show her emotions. She heard Ellie speaking to one of the townsfolk. "Do you know who that is?"

Elizabeth watched the exchange, wondering why the look of adoration appeared on everyone's face when they began to stare.

Slowly, some townsfolk stood. "It is him! I saw it in yesterdays paper."

"Who?" Elizabeth asked, confused.

"Why, it's all over the news. The Mill Ridge Journal put the story out yesterday. Didn't you read the paper, Elizabeth?"

"I, uh, no." She was ashamed to admit she bought the paper for her renters but was usually too busy to take time to read. Day old paper made good starter for the cook stove.

"You missed it then," Ellie noted. "I can't believe we are fortunate to have in our town the Texas Ranger who single-handedly took down the Riley Gang."

"Texas Ranger? Impressive." Even though she wasn't impressed. Where was the law when those outlaws wiped out everyone she had loved in her small Kansas town? She almost hated law men as much as she hated outlaws. Elizabeth should be ashamed of feeling so awful. The bitterness would eat her alive if she didn't keep it in check. No matter, she had to get back to help Rose with breakfast. The renters would be up and ready to be served by now.

"Have a good day, Nurse Ellie. Stop in for tea soon."

Nurse Ellie nodded, still staring at the stranger. Elizabeth shook her head, swinging around to see what the big deal was.

The horse was about two feet away. She noticed the Ranger's clothing first, as the horse was so tall she came face to face with the man's thigh. She needed him to move on so she could cross the street. When he stayed right there, she tried to keep her temper in check. "Oh for Pete sake, mister. Would you mind, I'm trying to cross the street."

Elizabeth's patience was running out. She hadn't realized she had dallied so long, it was important for her to do her job and make sure her guests were fed and on their way. She pulled the egg basket closer, gathered up her skirts with her free hand and stepped on to the street.

"Elizabeth," the raspy sound came from the man on the horse, its familiar lull causing her to raise her head in utter surprise.

Her head began to pound, the sound of his voice the only thing she understood. Voices in the background faded out. All Elizabeth saw was a pair of blue-gray eyes staring down at her.

His eyes.

The man she had loved with all her heart and soul.

She let the basket of eggs slide from her fingers. Some rolled from the basket, cracking as they hit the dirt ground.

Her heart felt as if it were pounding a mile a minute, her throat so tight she didn't have the capacity to speak. Shock overcame reality. She knew he was speaking to her, saw the motion of his mouth but had no clue how to make out the words he was saying. He began to slide from the big stallion, and yet she kept her eyes on his, like a magnet, as if she didn't dare break contact.

If she did, this would be a dream and she knew she'd wake up to realize it wasn't real.

Her throat became dry, her nostrils flared. She reached out, wanting to touch him so bad. Her body felt as if it were floating away from him instead of towards him, so she tried to grab him as he came closer. It didn't work, the clouds gathered around and pulled her away. "Noah," she whispered, his name on her lips as she fell into the darkness.

An Outlaw's [1]Honor[2] Available Now![3]

(https://www.amazon.com/Outlaws-Honor-Brides-Mill-Ridge-

ebook/dp/B0747BD5YY/

---

1. https://www.amazon.com/Outlaws-Honor-Brides-Mill-Ridge-

ebook/dp/B0747BD5YY/

ref=as_li_ss_tl?ie=UTF8&qid=1521047259&sr=8-

1&keywords=an+outlaws+honor&linkCode=ll1&tag=keysvac

a-20&linkId=9dfdfff4c484d3c0efb60c43c00eeb75

2. https://www.amazon.com/Outlaws-Honor-Brides-Mill-Ridge-

ebook/dp/B0747BD5YY/

ref=as_li_ss_tl?ie=UTF8&qid=1521047259&sr=8-

1&keywords=an+outlaws+honor&linkCode=ll1&tag=keysvac

a-20&linkId=9dfdfff4c484d3c0efb60c43c00eeb75

3. https://www.amazon.com/Outlaws-Honor-Brides-Mill-Ridge-

ebook/dp/B0747BD5YY/

ref=as_li_ss_tl?ie=UTF8&qid=1521047259&sr=8-

ref=as_li_ss_tl?ie=UTF8&qid=1521047259&sr=8-1&keywords=an+outlaws+honor&linkCode=ll1&tag=keysvaca-20&linkId=9dfdfff4c484d3c0efb60c43c00eeb75)

Don't miss out!

Visit the website below and you can sign up to receive emails whenever Cyndi Raye publishes a new book. There's no charge and no obligation.

https://books2read.com/r/B-A-PXQ-OCWFC

BOOKS 2 READ

Connecting independent readers to independent writers.